Libba's bitter hatred was shutting everyone out—even Daniel.

As Libba turned her back and isolated herself, Daniel pounded his fist against his thigh. Frustrated, he flung out, "Don't be foolish, Libba."

"Don't call me foolish!" Wringing her hands, she cried out in misery. "I hate Sherman, and oh, Daniel, I know it is heretical, but I hate my father!"

"But don't hate me! . . . Don't shut me out." He held out his arms. "Let me love you!"

She could hear a sharp edge in his voice warning her that even Daniel Marshall's infinite patience was wearing thin, but she eluded his reaching arms.

"I can't forgive my father for not loving me. What—oh, Daniel, what if we had a child, and I couldn't love it? You can't marry me. I'm only half a person!"

"Nonsense. Oh, Libba, think! Think about the love you and Nannie shared. You've had a tragic experience, but many people have suffered. God did not promise that we would not suffer, but that He could turn the suffering to—don't run away from me," he pleaded, hurting as badly as she.

"Libba," he called after her as she plunged up the stone steps. "Don't keep running in the wrong direction!"

JACQUELYN COOK is a veteran inspirational romance author whose extensive research brings alive the gracious living of the people of Macon, Georgia, during the late 1800s.

Books by Jacquelyn Cook

HEARTSONG PRESENTS

HP17—River of Fire

Beyond the Searching River

Jacquelyn Cook

Heartsong Presents

For
Anne Chichester Winship
who rode the rug
at Great Hill Place

ISBN 1-55748-399-X

BEYOND THE SEARCHING RIVER

PRINTED IN U.S.A.

one

Cinder-laden smoke spewed from the locomotive and obscured the scene of the wreck. Dazed, Libba Ramsey lay against the bank of red, Georgia clay like a rag doll tossed aside by a careless child. She scrubbed the turquoise ring on her clenched fist against an offending trickle of water tickling her cheek.

I never allow myself to cry? she questioned. She fought to remember. She had been sitting on the observation platform of the president's coach buttoning her shoe when the ballooning smokestack and pointed cowcatcher of a locomotive loomed through the haze of the September morning.

Blackness reclaimed her. She sank against the unyielding clay. Dreaming, she smelled, not clean wood smoke, but the sharp, penetrating odor of turpentine. Her dry eyes burned with the branding of the image of pine trees skinned by railroad tracks knotted around them like pretzels.

"That snake-eyed Sherman. I'll never forgive him!" Libba struggled up against the restraining hands of a young man bending over her squeezing water from his handkerchief.

"Wake up. The war is over, done," he said in a softly drawling voice. "It's Friday, September 15, 1876. Remember?" Gentle fingers soothed her thin shoulder. "One must forgive, forget."

Like a hurt puppy determined to get up, Libba

wriggled, raised her head, forced open intensely blue eyes. She did not lie in a flat, pine swamp. Hills covered in oaks and poplars surrounded her. The railroad tracks lay straight, sure of their destination rather than being grotesquely twisted.

The young man blinked gray-blue eyes as if he had just awakened and was delighted with what he had discovered. His tousled dark hair was streaked with gray, but as she watched an engaging grin chase the concern from his innocent, round face, she knew he could be only slightly older than the almost eighteen she thought herself to be.

Blushing, she straightened the bustle bent beneath her and raked her fingers through her wild tangle of curls which were as sooty black as the smut he had just washed from her face.

"For a minute I was six years old again," she explained. "Sherman's men burned Magnolia Springs. I fled through the piney woods to Savannah."

"You are no doubt fleeing from Savannah this time. The yellow fever epidemic? No wonder you're so plucky. You've done a lot of escaping for one so young." He waved his arms in wide gestures as he talked, adding further punctuation to his expressive voice. "Who are you? Where are you running *to*?"

She shook her head. "Nobody," she said huskily. Choking on emotion, she could say no more. She could not tell this kind young man that she barely knew who she was. She lowered thick, dark lashes lest he see the secret pain that blinded her from her uncertain searching.

Daniel Marshall thought her clear blue eyes the most enchanting he had ever seen. They dominated a face white as porcelain. Her pointed chin trembled momentarily only to firm with determination. When he had jumped from the train to take her out of harm's way, he had thought her a child. Indeed, she probably weighed less than ninety pounds. When he scooped her into his arms, he felt her shoulder blades protruding, fragile as a bird's wing. But she was unmistakably emerging into womanhood. Daniel was surprised at his longing to continue to hold her, to shelter her from whatever it was that he had glimpsed in her eyes.

Suddenly self-conscious, he slapped short fingers to his face pulling down the corners of his eyes and mouth to make a mask of tragedy. Lowering his voice to a comic exaggeration, he intoned, "You'll feel better if you cry."

Libba jutted her chin. "I never cry. What happened?" Glazing her eyes against him, she slid her hand over a patch on her skirt while he absorbed her rebuff before replying.

"The car at the end broke loose from the rest of the train. The freight following slammed into it. The jolt must have thrown you clear. Where were you?"

"Oh! Is everyone all right. I must help." Forgetting herself, Libba tried to stand, but her knees gave way when she saw that the locomotive, W.M. Wadley, was spewing steam into the Colonel's private car.

Its brass bell belatedly tolling brought chattering passengers spilling from the coaches. Men dressed in long, flapping coattails discussed the delays of the rail accident, still a common occurrence in these modern days.

Women, upholstered in the odd, goose-shaped silhouette of the day—narrow skirts pulled back into heavily adorned bustles and enormous, plumed Gainsborough hats—were excitedly taking part in the scene as they exercised their new freedom, both from cumbersome hoop skirts and from restrictive prewar mores. All, however, were properly hatted and gloved even at this early hour. Libba was suddenly aware that she was not, and, worse, she was allowing a strange man to talk with her.

She forgot herself again when she spotted the striking figure of a broad-shouldered man, calm in spite of the confusion of everyone else. Laboring along with the crew to right the wreck was the man for whom the engine was named. Unhatted, crowned with thick white hair, Colonel Wadley towered above the rest. With the erect carriage of his six-foot, one-inch frame clothed in perfectly tailored, plum-colored alpaca and with his aristocratic bearing, William Morrill Wadley was a man in charge. He was oblivious to the escaping steam hissing around his ankles from behind the cowcatcher of the locomotive, built to honor him more than twenty years ago when he was merely superintendent of the Central Rail Road and Banking Company. In a crisp, New Hampshire twang, he barked curt orders which he expected to be followed to the letter. Abruptly, he turned and came striding toward them.

Daniel's graying eyebrows lifted at the corners as he spoke in an awe-struck whisper. "Do you know who that is?" He hurriedly smoothed his rumpled, threadbare, blue serge suit. "He's Colonel Wadley, president of the Central. He's been called the ablest railroad official in the South. He was superintendent of the railroads of the Confederacy." He deepened his voice to a rumble and the outside corners of his eyebrows went up as he made a wry face and added, "Even though he was born a Yankee." Changing back to his natural grin, he added respectfully, "He's the man who put the railroads back together after the war."

Libba stood on wobbly knees as Wadley and his statuesque, auburn-haired wife approached.

"Luther Elizabeth are you hurt?" Mrs. Wadley reached out to Libba. The pupils of her bright, yellow-hazel eyes enlarged at the bump on Libba's forehead. "Mr. Wadley," she said to her husband in formal address, reflecting her Savannah upbringing. "This child is hurt!"

"I . . . I'm fine, Miss Rebecca," Libba stammered.

Daniel Marshall opened his mouth in surprise. Puffing out his smooth cheeks, he let his vulnerable face fall slack as he moved aside deferentially for the patrician gentleman. If this girl was Wadley's daughter, what chance did he have to woo her? He had only a crumbling mansion and a mother to provide for. He had sprung into manhood early in those terrible days during the Reconstruction. People knew that the war was over and something must be done to make a living, but there was nothing with which to start. From his mother he had received a good brain and a strong faith which enabled him to reach deep within himself for the strength and courage to continue when the future held no promise. Now, faced with the commanding presence of Wadley, whose name was in the South equivalent with that in the East of New York Central tycoon Cornelius Vanderbilt, he felt his courage draining. Castigating himself for cowardice, Daniel Marshall backed away.

Wadley bent to examine Libba's injury, thankful that his wife's latest object of charity was not critically hurt. Wadley had been sitting at the rear of the car when he looked up and saw the engine coming. He remembered nothing else until he found himself on the side of the road not knowing how he had gotten out. The loose car had been stopped by the action of automatic air brakes, but the freight train which was following had smashed nearly to the berths where his family lay sleeping.

With a soothing touch, surprising in so large and muscular a man, Colonel Wadley assisted Libba back aboard a Pullman car.

A dense cloud of black smoke rose above the waiting passenger engine, R.R. Cuyler. Two long blasts from the whistle, the signal to release brakes and proceed, jarred Libba's teeth and made her wonder if the whole earth were shaking. The bell began to clang. She turned to say thank you, but her Samaritan was gone.

Lying in a berth, lulled by the soft *choo-choo-choo* of the rolling train, Libba submitted gratefully as Rebecca Wadley sponged her cuts. Gazing soberly at this plain woman who had such laughing eyes, Libba reflected on her good fortune in meeting these wonderful people when Wadley had come as the president of the Union Society, the charitable club which oversaw Bethesda Orphanage for boys. His wife had meanwhile inspected the girls' branch, the Savannah Female Asylum. Libba had lived there in austere poverty with her mind mercifully blotting out her past.

In the strict, religious atmosphere, she had survived. She had tried to put a little fun in the other orphans' existence. Something in Libba's indomitable spirit had captured the attention of the motherly Mrs. Wadley.

Yellow fever had broken out in August of 1876. By mid-September, the cemeteries could not hold the corpses with emaciated frames and strangely yellow faces. No one knew the cause of the dreadful scourge. Whispering that the epidemic must have come in on filthy foreign ships, people fled the seashore.

Libba had thought only that the young usually survived and she would again—but for what? From some unsearchable distance, God had perhaps ordained that fortune smile for a time upon her. The Wadleys had invited her to visit their cotton plantation in the uplands of Monroe County, Georgia.

The swaying of her berth lessened as the *bum-bump, bum-bump* of the train over the rails slowed. The whistle blasted one long, mournful ummmmmm to indicate it was approaching Georgia's central city, Macon. It was only an overnight trip from the seacoast since Colonel Wadley had consolidated lines and accelerated passenger service. Built during the slow, easy romance of the steamboat era, Macon had seen its river trade dwindle; however, town planners had moved quickly to push rail lines beyond the river, north above the fall line, southwest through cotton land. Now the rail center of the whole southeast, Macon recognized William Wadley as the unquestioned genius behind its economic power.

"Macon! Ma-con, Ge-or-gia," called the conductor.

Ssssst! With steam escaping, the train rattled, jolted to a screaking stop. Looking out of the window, Libba saw the young man. With springing steps and laughing asides to fellow passengers, he bounded away.

Oh! she thought. *I didn't thank him. I don't even know his name. I'll never see him again!*

With a longing emptiness, she remembered the way the outside corners of his eyebrows had gone up from his little-boy eyes as he talked in funny voices trying to make her laugh. Sighing forlornly because love was an unknown quantity in her life, she dabbed at a blur in her eye. Turning her mouth down bitterly, she mumbled resolutely, "Just a cinder."

Rolling over painfully, she saw that Rebecca Wadley was putting away her wash basin, sponge, and salve.

"Bolingbroke is only fifteen miles north of Macon." Mrs. Wadley's soft voice drawled the words into extra syllables. "Are you able to get up?"

"Yes, ma'am," Libba said staunchly.

Carriages waited at the depot in Bolingbroke. Libba was swept along with a flurry as passengers and baggage were transferred. A short distance from the railroad, they approached a simple, dignified entrance guarded by massive, acrid-smelling boxwoods. Wrought-iron gates swung wide, welcoming them into Great Hill Place.

The carriages swayed along a winding lane through the cool greenness of damp, natural woodland. Libba breathed fragrant cedar, cleansing after the smoke from the wood-burning locomotive. Towering over everything were the oaks. Accustomed to low, spreading live oaks of the coast, Libba gazed up, up at these stalwart sentinels which seemed to echo the Wadley's promise of beneficent protection.

With her cloak of stoic acceptance sliding from around her, Libba was transformed by the tranquillity. Thirstily, she drank in the beauty, the peace, the vibrancy. Pines whispered. Mockingbirds trilled melodious tunes. Squirrels and chipmunks scampered unafraid over the rustling brown carpet of pine straw. Slender hardwoods trembled in the newly cool breeze, waiting eagerly for a finger of frost to stroke them into living flames.

The joy of homecoming made the family lean forward as they approached the house through a lane of black-green pyramids of magnolias glistening in the setting sun. Silence burst as dogs came loping from all directions, barking a welcoming chorus. Fine hunting dogs wagging tails, huge mongrels wagging bodies, and one tailless mutt hopping gamely on three legs were joined by whooping children to form a parade to the house.

"Ahhh!" Libba glimpsed Great Hill Place. She had feared overwhelming grandeur; instead, the white frame house shouldered sheltering oaks and spreading camellias and stood as contentedly among the surrounding boxwoods as stately Mrs. Wadley now stood with grand-children nudging her skirts.

A gabled stoop extending from the porch gave an odd, friendly look. Suddenly more sons, daughters, and various spouses spilled around them. The Wadleys had had nine children (seven now living), and Libba laughed helplessly at trying to sort them out. The warmth of their greeting made Libba feel, for the first time in her life, at home.

Supper was a feast. Salty-peppery fried ham and meat-seasoned peas and beans awakened Libba's taste buds. She thought the meat course was completed, but the white-haired man who served the table offered her a huge tureen with chunks of chicken and dumplings swimming in butter. Declaring they must fatten her up and put color in her cheeks, everyone pressed Libba to take second helpings. When hot scuppernong cobbler with whipped cream sliding into melting pools was placed before her, she ate slowly, resting between spoonfuls.

"Enough!" Libba held up her hands in defeat. "It's wonderful, but I can't eat another bite!"

Her smile included the butler, Prince. He returned her look with a scowl that bristled the white eyebrows standing out from his dark face and soured his bulldog jowls. Plainly he thought that she was not the social equal of this family whom he had remained a part of in spite of the Emancipation. Libba's wariness returned. Even here, her mettle would be tested.

Libba had dropped her guard for a moment, and Rebecca Wadley saw the pain in her clear blue eyes.

"Sarah Lois, take this exhausted child to her room."

From the sea of faces, one emerged, solicitous, kind. Arresting brown eyes that snapped with intelligence from beneath straight dark brows kept the solemn face from being plain. The eldest daughter, now thirty-two, was the undisputed chatelaine in her mother's stead. Resigned to spinsterhood, she lived through the lives of others. On her twenty-fourth birthday, she had passed the marriageable age, but she had not let being an old maid quell her zest for living. Looking at Libba, she murmured for her to follow.

Libba tried not to stare at the odd lace cap Sarah Lois wore over her severely parted auburn hair. Long lace strips, which hung from each side of the cap and lay in folds on Sarah Lois's broad shoulders, swung as she climbed the stairs. Libba winced as stabs of pain reminded her that she had been thrown from the train.

Sarah Lois opened wide a door. "This is your room."

"Mine?" Libba asked in squeaky-voiced surprise. "You mean a room all to myself?" Timidly, Libba stepped across a cool bare floor of mirror-polished oak.

"Yes, of course. For as long as you—need it. Let me know if I can get you anything." The sweet-faced woman softly closed the door.

Alone! What luxury! For a long moment Libba stood perfectly still, absorbing the quietness. Dominating the room was a bed of rosewood, four posted, carved in the most exquisite and intricate pineapple design. *It is far too beautiful to sleep on*, she thought. *I ought to lie awake and simply enjoy looking at it*. A matching rosewood dresser and cheval glass stood on either side of the bed. The mirror showed her tiredness.

Removing her drab traveling attire, Libba untied her bustle petticoat with its poufs of muslin which covered the steel hoops of her badly bent bustle. Splashing water into the porcelain bowl from the matching cabbage-rose-painted pitcher on the marble-topped wash stand, she scrubbed off the grime from the train trip and put on an often-darned muslin gown.

She knelt beside the bedskirts as she had been taught to kneel beside her cot and intoned a prayer with little thought that her words were heard.

Twisting the turquoise ring on her finger, Libba realized that the Wadleys were right: she was thin. Fearing her one treasure would be lost, she placed it on the gold chain about her neck as it had been in her earliest recollection.

Stepping on the needlepoint-covered stool, she climbed onto the bed piled high with a multitude of mattresses. Slightly dizzy, she clung to the top feather mattress, feeling as if she might fall off. She had never slept so high. She lay staring wide-eyed at the white muslin canopy, envisioning the engaging grin of the gentle young man. He had called her plucky. Well, she was used to taking knocks. She had escaped death once more, but for what? Biting her lips, she fought despair and hopelessness of what lay beyond this brief respite.

Her fingers closed on the large, Victorian ring. Her thumb rubbed the smooth oval turquoise and pressed one of the carved gold flowers surrounding it. A hidden spring snapped. With blue eyes determinedly tearless, she gazed into the glass-covered compartment which held the only clue to her place in the world.

two

Birds singing in the magnolia tree outside her window awakened Libba at daybreak.

"Ohhh-um," she groaned as she tried to turn her aching body in the puff of the feather mattress. Wishing she could bury her head under the goosedown pillow and never get up, she lay for a moment submerged in misery, then, determinedly, slid down from the bed.

She must be useful if she were to be welcome here. Summoning every ounce of strength, she pulled her brown calico dress over her stiff shoulders.

Descending the mahogany-railed staircase, Libba paused uncertainly and looked down from the landing. Everything about the house had an uncluttered elegance, a simple dignity with nothing calculated to impress. Rococo styles were popular, but the Wadleys preferred genuineness.

The rumble of a coffee grinder told Libba someone was up before her. The delicious scent of bacon frying drew her across the hall to the rear of the house.

Stepping into a tremendous kitchen, she blinked, trying to sort out the blur of color and the bustle of activity. Hanging from the exposed rafters of the high ceiling were strings of peppers: red, yellow, green. Drying herbs added nose-twitching aromas. Several women worked busily, laughing, chattering.

"Good morning," said Libba tentatively.

A chorus of welcome greeted her. Mrs. Wadley strode

forward and lifted the black curls with which Libba had carefully concealed her forehead.

"How are you feeling, Luther Elizabeth," she asked as she mashed the purple lump.

"Fine, ma'am." Libba swallowed pain and curtsied.

Rebecca Wadley's pupils enlarged as she probed Libba's guarded eyes. Without comment, she ladled steaming oatmeal into an earthenware bowl and sprinkled it generously with brown sugar. Handing it to Libba, she said, "Come with me."

Wonderingly, Libba followed outside, down steep steps, and across the yard to a small house. Coolness kissed her cheeks as she stepped inside the thick brick walls. They were inside a creamery lined with cold-holding marble shelves keeping pitchers of milk and pans of cream.

Mrs. Wadley dipped a ladle into the thick golden cream and placed a huge dollop on Libba's oatmeal.

Mouth watering, Libba tasted the sweet hot cereal and cool cream. "Delicious! Sheer bliss."

"Now, I want you to rest and relax all day," Rebecca commanded .

"No, ma'am. I'm used to working. Jus' give me a job, and—"

"Tomorrow, maybe. Not today."

As they stepped back into the warm sunshine, Sarah Lois emerged from the other side of the creamery building. Through a heavy iron door that looked like a bank vault, Libba glimpsed a windowless room, dark save for sunbeams slipping through the slits where an occasional brick had been left out to provide ventilation. A huge iron safe hunched in one corner half-hidden by wooden barrels marked Flour and Sugar. Sarah Lois selected a key from the heavy ring she wore dangling from a chain around her waist and carefully locked the door.

They returned to the kitchen where Sarah Lois distributed the measured ingredients to the servants for the day's menu. Rebecca, herself, wiped every breakfast dish.

Libba ate ravenously. As her gnawing stomach began to fill, she nibbled a hot, fluffy biscuit dripping with sticky pear preserves and pondered what she saw. Servants moved out in all directions. She was not needed here any more than she had been at the orphanage. Because she had graduated as the pupil with highest honors, she had been appointed as a teacher; but with so many deaths from yellow fever, she had simply become an unwanted mouth to feed. Libba did not know why, seeing her, Rebecca had opened her great heart in compassion and asked her husband to become Libba's guardian. She did know that she was approaching the age when she must find a place for herself.

Screams interrupted her dark thoughts. Squeals, peals of laughter drew her to the center hall. Two small boys and a girl were taking turns riding a throw rug. While the others cheered, one doubled down, took a running start, flopped stomach down on the rug, and glided down the highly waxed oak floor from the back door to the front.

The freckled-faced girl tugged at Libba's hand. "Come on. Do a bellywhopper."

"I've never seen anything that looked like so much fun," whispered Libba wistfully. She eyed the Tiffany lamp teetering on a marble-topped table in the entry. Chairs marched around the walls with backs as stiff and ramrod straight as the people in this family. "Won't you get in trouble?"

"No. It's allowed," assured a dark-haired boy with a full, sensitive mouth. "But remember, we can't run anywhere in the house except the hall. Try it."

Libba looked at the portraits on the wall: a stern Colonel Wadley, an imposing General Lee, and a mocking Mona Lisa. Shivering between fear and temptation, she jerked a nod and gathered up her floor-length skirt, which she had only recently started wearing to set her apart from the children. She had not fooled this group. They knew a fellow tomboy when they saw one. Running a few steps, she flopped on the rug. Whizzing down the polished floor past the clapping, yelling children, she raised her head triumphantly just in time to see the front door looming. It opened. The rug sailed across the porch and skidded to a stop at the edge of the stoop.

"Do you try to break that swanlike neck at least once a day?" a deep, virile voice inquired, chuckling.

Mortified, Libba lay face down, unmoving. She cringed at the sight of two large, well-shined boots. *Maybe if I die they will go away.*

"Are you all right?" The male laughter turned to alarm at her stillness. Strong hands lifted her shoulders.

"Yes, sir," murmured Libba. "That was a foolish thing to do—especially after yesterday." She threw back her head to look at the dark-haired man. *Why did it have to be the handsomest one in the family who caught me?*

Suddenly she burst out laughing. "It was fun!"

His rich laughter joined hers as he helped her to one of the white wicker porch chairs. "It's a good thing they added the stoop or you'd have gone bumping down the steps like—"

Grasping at a change of subject, Libba replied, "I don't believe I've ever seen a porch with a stoop, Mr. . . . . I'm so sorry. I met so many of you last night, I've forgotten."

"Paul Morley," he said, looking disappointed that he had not made more of an impression. He sat on the swing at one end of the porch and surveyed her. "Paul," he repeated. "Don't call me mister. I'm just kinfolks—here for a visit. But to answer your question, Cousin William is of Puritan ancestry. Now, Cousin Rebecca is a daughter of the Old South." His brown eyes twinkled as he tweaked his dark mustache and smiled with calculated charm.

"When they moved here after the war and began remodeling this old house, Cousin William assembled the family and asked if they wanted a southern porch or a northern stoop. The vote was a tie, so he built both. The house is a strange mix. Perhaps we all are, too."

Libba had feared that her silly display would make him think her a child, but as the swing rocked, he roamed his eyes up and down her with the motion, clearly assessing her a woman. Her insides jerked and bumped like a train zigzagging down a crooked track.

Oooummmm! The shattering whistle seemed a part of her emotions, but it brought a clattering of footsteps. Children tumbled off the stoop and galloped down the lane.

"They're catching the train to school," Paul explained, relaxing his spell upon her. "And I'd better get to work. I'm designing a system to give the house running water—you can come see if you like."

Unaccustomed to talking with a man at all, much less

one this handsome, Libba felt relief at the interruption. Cautioning herself that she must be better armed for his overwhelming virility, she refused. "Thank you, no. But perhaps tomorrow." She fanned back her thick lashes from her clear blue eyes and gave him her most charming smile. "For now, I'm going to obey Miss Rebecca's command and rest."

Paul grinned agreeably. "Good idea. Why don't you help yourself to the library." He tipped a wide-brimmed straw hat and went down the steps two at a time.

Libba went back into the house, empty now, quiet. From the library's well-stocked shelves, she selected a slim volume of poetry, *Sonnets From The Portuguese*. The oak-paneled library seemed as imposing as Colonel Wadley himself, and Libba hoped it was permitted to take the books from the room. A door opening on a side porch provided escape.

Pale sunshine filtered the mists of a sky that looked like scrubbed pewter. The breeze was cool, refreshing after the steaming heat of summer in Savannah. Here in the hills of middle Georgia, summer-parched earth had been revived by September gales, and lush green overflowed the yard and the meadow beyond. In the distance, she could see cotton fields white unto harvest.

The pungent smell of boxwood invited Libba toward a formal garden. For a moment she stood at the entrance and looked down a series of terraces. A flower bed several levels down seemed alive with bobbing heads of surprise lilies awakened by the recent rains. Popped up on their nearly invisible, leafless stems, they looked like so many red spiders suspended knee-high. Libba was tempted to follow the walk which wound into mysterious, unseen depths. Intrigued, she wanted to explore, but a terrible weariness, a feeling that she had been beaten by a heavy rod, made her decide to wait.

A prickling sensation that she was not alone made her glance overhead. A girl about her own age lay entwined along a smooth, flat limb of a mimosa tree with her nose in a book. Moving softly lest she disturb her, Libba turned toward the kitchen yard.

A tall, turbaned woman was sweeping the red clay with a broom made of branches from wild dog fennel bushes. Libba greeted her pleasantly, "Good morning."

The servant returned her "Good morning" sympathetically, but as soon as Libba passed, the woman began to talk as though the girl could not hear with her back turned.

"Po' little critter. So thin and hongry a puff of wind could blow her away."

"Humph. A lot you know," a man's voice replied. "She eats a sight. So much it makes her po' to tote it."

Squaring her shoulders, Libba marched up a hill toward a hammock strung between two elms. The hillcrest was a delightful suspension between the inhabited yard and the meadow rolling away in every direction with an open invitation to roam, to lie among the daisies, and dream. Away on the next rise, a vaulted brick tower stood guarding the meadow. For what strange purpose? It excited Libba's imagination, but aching legs made her stop at the hammock.

She stretched out luxuriously. Swinging gently, lulled by birdsongs, she let the joy, the peace of the atmosphere soothe her troubled spirit. For a few moments she would allow herself to pretend she was somebody, a real person who belonged on this beautiful plantation, isolated from the world's harsh reality.

Idly, she read a few pages, but her eyelids became heavy. Drifting into dream-troubled sleep, she tossed, wrestled, set the hammock wildly rocking.

"No!" she screamed. "Don't let them see you. They'll kill us—or worse!" She flung the book. The ringing of hammers, the penetrating smell of turpentine, the grotesque image of iron rails knotted around pine trees, the searing heat of a roaring fire: all of her nightmare returned.

With a sudden bump, Libba awakened. Dumped on her bustle again, she sat with the netting of the hammock wrapped about her head. Struggling free, she looked about furtively. The ringing of the hammers was real. Workman were adding a wing, apartments for William Oconius Wadley and his family while they built a home.

No one seemed to have witnessed her latest tumble. Getting up gingerly, she started for the house.

The book! She limped back. Her welcome would certainly be revoked if she left that fine leather volume on the ground.

She took refuge in her room. At noon there was a knock on her door. Sarah Lois peered in, wearing, as usual, her odd lace cap and her enigmatic smile. "I brought you a tray," she said. "Endine told me you took another fall. You just stay in bed all afternoon until you get over being shaky."

"You're too kind to me," Libba protested. She sipped a swallow of buttermilk and attacked the laden plate. Who was Endine and which show of stupidity had she witnessed?

Her stomach full, she began to read Elizabeth Barrett Browning's Sonnet I:

> *And a voice said in mastery while I strove, . . .*
> *"Guess now who holds thee?"—"Death," I said.*
>   *But there,*
> *The silver answer rang. . . "Not Death, but Love."*

She envisioned a tousled head, a pair of gray-blue eyes brimming with concern. She cupped her hand around her cheek and felt again a gentle touch, heard a warm voice saying, "It's over. Forgive. Forget."

A bittersweet longing made her wish that she could laugh with the good-natured clowning of that interesting young man. She realized that he had been awed when the prominent Wadleys greeted her familiarly. He had retreated. Sighing, Libba commanded herself to stop dreaming. She would never see him again.

When the afternoon shadows stretched across the shining floor, Libba's natural determination gained victory over her shakiness. She slid down from the high bed.

Silk was not in her wardrobe. Her Sunday gingham with its crocheted collar hung alone in the vastness of the mahogany armoire. Brushing her black curls furiously, she left them as wild a tumble as if she had been running in the wind.

Stepping into the hall, she encountered the girl she had seen reading in the mimosa. Her hair was as faded pink, as fine and frizzy as a mimosa blossom; her face was as freckled as if it had been pasted with the big brown seeds. Because she had neither the beauty nor the dignity of the other family members, Libba dropped her guard, smiled, admiring one who did not think herself too old or too grand to climb a tree. "Hello. You're . . . ?"

"Endine," the girl supplied.

"Ahn—"

"Deen. It's spelled E-n-d-i-n-e, but it's pronounced like a doctor told you to say ah, then sneeze." She laughed.

Happiness warmed Libba. This was Paul's sister. Perhaps she had found a friend.

"My name is Elizabeth, but there was a child who could only lisp out Libba and that stuck."

Endine linked Libba's arm through hers and guided her through the back hall to join the rest of the family assembling in the large, stiffly formal dining room. Although the ladies had not dressed elaborately, they were fresh, clean, smelling of lavender sachet. Each one held her carefully groomed head in a certain way as she walked gracefully across the room and seated herself properly into her chair by a rule which escaped Libba. As Paul held back a chair for her, Libba fumbled, forgetting which side of the chair to enter.

Looking up and down the long table, Libba tried to identify the rest of the family, sons and daughters and their families with numerous children named for their grandparents. All of the Wadley's were tall and had patrician noses, masses of auburn hair, and eyes that arrested one with a glance. Oh, she would never keep them straight, especially since there were so many of them carrying on the important family names.

Nervously watching Mrs. Wadley to see which fork to take, Libba ate something that she guessed was an artichoke. Under the butler's scrutiny, she determined not to eat piggishly as she had done the night before. She jumped when she heard her name.

"Libba's trying to break every bone in her body," Endine said. "She fell out of the hammock screaming about pretzels."

Pinioned by Endine's yellow eyes, Libba clutched the ring dangling on its gold chain about her neck. A forced laugh gurgled in her throat. "I have an unexplainable nightmare. It's impossible, but railroad tracks are twisted around pine trees, and. . . ." Her voice trailed away.

Brown eyes in blank faces stared at her from motionless bodies up and down the long table.

Endine's freckles seemed to stand out from her face as she curled her thin lip in a sneer. "Just who are you, anyway?"

three

Biting the turquoise ring, Libba shrank from Endine's unexpected enmity. Suddenly she threw back her dark cloud of hair and stared, unblinking, at her freckle-faced challenger.

"I can't really say." Her voice cracked, but she continued. "I know I'm a Southerner because I'll always hate blue cloth!"

"I know Libba's a southern *lady* because she has such tiny feet," Paul said, kicking his sister's large shoe. "Did you know the Chinese marry a little-footed wife and then take a big-footed wife to be her slave?"

The others made a show of eating, but Colonel Wadley put down his fork and fixed his piercing eyes upon Endine. At first the girl glared back at him in defiance, but as his lower lip protruded sternly, she mumbled a half-hearted apology.

Wadley's handsome face remained set in its usual grave expression, but his hazel eyes softened with kindness as he turned to Libba who was angrily crumbling a piece of corn bread.

"I've seen your nightmare."

Heedlessly dropping her bread, Libba stared at him.

Wadley continued in his crisp, terse twang. "I recall the rails looped around pines like pretzels. I still feel the heat of anger." His mouth twisted bitterly. "It's no wonder a child would be permanently marked by such horror."

All eyes turned toward him. With a self-conscious laugh, he resumed speaking in a gentler tone.

"Sometimes when the source of a nightmare is explained, the dream will cease." He settled back in his chair with laced fingers resting on his vest. "When the unfortunate War Between the States ended, this family was, of course, heartbroken, penniless, destitute of clothing save for coarsest homespun. We were living in Louisiana at the time. Life was a shambles. No work. The finances of the Vicksburg, Shreveport, and Texas Railroad Company did not admit of repairing the ruined road."

Libba shifted. What had all this to do with her dreams? Could he really help her find herself?

"A man of fifty-two with seven children, I was without a dollar. I decided to seek refuge from United States rule by moving us to Brazil to rehabilitate my fortunes.

"Then on the hottest day in July—it was 1865—I was working in my blacksmith shop when Mr. Courvoisie arrived from Savannah bearing a letter asking me to return to Georgia to restore the ruined railroad. It was nothing but twisted track and burned bridges."

Mrs. Wadley glowed. "The letter said Mr. Wadley's knowledge, ability, and energy could rebuild the railroads better than anyone."

"Eagerly, I started for Georgia by going on a steamboat down the Mississippi to New Orleans. The South was so utterly devastated it would have taken months to cross it. The quickest way to reach Savannah was by way of Chicago, Niagara Falls, New York City, and thence by steamship to Savannah. I reached there in exactly one month."

"But, Papa!" protested John, reddening because his voice changed. "You haven't explained Libba's nightmare."

"I'm coming to that! What I found in Georgia was this: General Sherman left Atlanta such a burning holocaust that one man said he could read his watch at midnight ten miles away. The Yankees marched across Georgia to the sea. Sherman's "bummers" destroyed everything in their path, but their special prey was the railroads. Sherman bragged he had done the state of Georgia damage of $100,000,000 with twenty million advantage to Union forces and the rest waste and destruction."

Tension crackled as the older ones relived the anguish.

Wadley's voice seemed to echo into the silence. "Luther Elizabeth, don't you remember anything about what happened to you? Where your home was located?"

A sad-eyed waif, Libba shook her head, unable to speak.

"I hazard you witnessed the destruction of the rails. With fiendish glee, Sherman's troops built bonfires of crossties, heated the middle of the rails red hot, and twisted them around trees. They destroyed three hundred miles of railroad."

Clenching her fists against her face to stifle a scream, Libba thought, *Three hundred miles! It's hopeless! I'll never find my home!* Bereavement drained her as if she had just been dealt the wrenching.

Rebecca Wadley's understanding softened her plain features. She got up and walked around the table to embrace Libba's hunched shoulders. "You have a home now, dear—and a family."

Libba longed to throw herself against Mrs. Wadley and sob out her wretchedness, but Endine's cold glare made her swallow the ache in her throat and renew her vow: *I'll never let myself cry.*

"Come, everyone!" Sarah Lois spoke in a voice that commanded attention. "What Libba needs is fun! Let's all go into the parlor and play—"

"Charades!"

"Funny recitations!"

"Dumbo crambo!"

Libba struggled to smile as grandchildren sprang to life with happy shouting and good-natured shoving for supremacy. A tingle of warmth penetrated her misery, and she looked up through a fan of dark lashes at Paul bending over her.

His spreading smile slowed, slipping into an expression of beguilement at her piquancy. With urging fingers on her elbow, he drew her up. "Come," he said in a voice meant only for her ears. "I'll teach you to play backgammon."

With a stiff shoulder toward Endine's sly looks, Libba preceded Paul into the parlor. Before he could unfold the wooden gameboard, sixteen-year-old John claimed her attention.

"I wanted to show you something." John smiled shyly and thrust a brass-bound mahogany tube into Libba's hand.

"What?" Libba began wonderingly. The foot-long piece was beautifully made, but she could not fathom its use.

"You've never seen a kaleidoscope?" John asked gleefully. "They are the latest rage in parlor entertainment."

"But what—"

Both men vied to clasp their hands over hers around the cylinder and tilt it toward the lamp.

Libba peeped into the end as they indicated. Sparkling, multi-colored bits reflected by mirrors formed a many-faceted design. Fascinated, she turned the kaleidoscope as directed and watched the tumbling pieces patterning endlessly.

John leaned adoringly over her shoulder. His hollow-cheeked face glowed red with the pleasure of making her smile. Paul reared back with his hands behind his head and heaved a sophisticated snort of boredom as the children began to clap and chant.

"Auntie, do 'Miss Fanny,' do 'Miss Fanny.'"

The dignified, austere Sarah Lois stood in the center of the parlor and recited a dialogue, changing her voice and making broad gestures which jiggled the white lace streamers of her house-cap.

The children screamed and shouted at the solemn old maid aunt who was jumping up and down and grabbing her legs against an imaginary whipping.

"Yes'm, Mama. Yes'm, Mama. I'm going back to church every Sunday," she screeched in a high-pitched voice. She danced from more blows of an *almost* visibly flapping strap.

"Yes'm, Mama. I'm gone read my Bible from lid to lid."

Waiting for the giggling to die down, she delivered the anticipated climax in the voice of the mother. "I tell you, Miss Fanny, I can make more Christians out of sinners with my old trunk strap than a preacher can in forty lebben years."

Applause filled the room. Endine jumped up to take center stage. With tossing pink hair, she recited:

> *Whatever I do; whatever I say,*
> *Aunt Sophie says it isn't the way.*
> *When she was a girl (forty summers ago);*
> *Aunt Sophie says they never did so.*

Endine shook a meaningful finger at Libba sandwiched between John and Paul and continued:

> *If I take a lad's arm—just for safety you know—*
> *Aunt Sophie says they never did so....*

Self-consciously, Libba drew away from the cousins. The changing voices and gestures of the recitations brought back an image of the young man at the wreck. She did wish she had thanked him.

Bong! Bong! The grandfather clock in the hall was striking ten, bedtime.

Mounting the stairs, Libba reached the turning and looked down as Endine's red head came conspiratorially close to Paul.

"You're as cow-eyed over her as John," Endine hissed. "You're the most eligible bachelor in the state of Georgia. Don't get mixed up with a nobody!"

Tears stung Libba's eyes, but she blinked them back. In the orphanages everyone had suffered from the war. They had never talked about what was past. She had never allowed herself to think about who she might be. She had sought only to make each day as bright as possible for the children in her charge and work herself tired enough to sleep without her nightmare. Now Endine's needling pricked her very soul.

Squeezing her ring, she stood in the shadows until everyone had drifted away. Summoning every ounce of her courage, she stole back down the stairs.

Because the dignified gentleman had not joined his children in the parlor games, Libba had assumed Colonel Wadley must have retired to the solitude of his study. Her timid knock went unanswered. Raking her hair away from her face, she drew a tremulous breath and rapped smartly.

"Come."

The terse voice weakened her knees. Wanting to bolt, Libba resolutely opened the door.

The air was redolent of richly oiled leathers. The room spoke one word: railroads. Lining the walls were lithographs of locomotives beginning with the first crude 1820s steam machines pulling carriages and ending with the contemporary, handsomely painted engines and coal cars of the 1870s. In a prominent place was a picture of the W.M. Wadley. A kerosene lamp cast a yellow glow over the man who looked splendid even at this hour in his white, winged collar and dark suit. He cocked one appraising eye from the report he was reading and fastened it sharply upon the slender girl who swayed like a milkweed pod poised before a puff of wind.

Libba cleared her throat. "Colonel Wadley, sir. I . . . I don't mean to bother you, sir. You've probably saved my life bringing me here, but . . . but . . . ." She whacked the heel of her hand at the black curls tumbling in her eyes and winced as she mashed the bruise on her forehead. She felt angry at herself for stammering, but she was not used to talking to men.

"It's probably hopeless to find my home. I've never worried too much before, but. . . ." Before her courage left her entirely, she finished in a rush. "Could you, please, help me find out who I am?"

Colonel Wadley's black brows came together. "You are what you make of yourself, young lady." His massive jaws set firmly as he fixed her with piercing eyes. "This is Endine's work. I shall reprimand her."

Lacing his fingers across his muscular chest he surveyed her. "I came down from New Hampshire with my anvil on my back. I may remark that with nothing but my God-given talent as a blacksmith I rose to an honored position with the railroad. You may, therefore, understand why, when the war destroyed everything any of us owned, I started again."

Libba feared to remind him that even though the late war had opened a few jobs for a respectable woman there was almost no opportunity outside of marriage.

Wadley relaxed his bushy eyebrows and dipped a big finger toward a chair. "Sit. Sit."

Libba obeyed, perching on the edge of the leather seat bending over rocking.

Wadley forced himself to speak gently. "I do understand what it's like to be fatherless. I liked nothing better than working iron with my father in his blacksmith shop—I made my first pair of pincers at the age of six. But he died when was thirteen. I became a blacksmith's apprentice."

Libba settled back in the chair as his voice droned.

Wadley told her how he had left New Hampshire in 1833 to seek his fortune in Savannah. He worked for only a few days as a fifty-cents-a-day forge striker before he began to rise from one position to the next. With encouragement from his high-born wife, he moved upward to superintendent of the Central Rail Road. By 1852, he was Georgia's recognized railroad expert. By 1861, he was accepted as the ablest railroad official in the South.

War came, destroying everything he had built. Recalling this, he sat unmoving. The ticking of the clock in the hallway intruded into their silence. Libba waited, afraid to breathe until he remembered her again.

"Perhaps you'll understand the reason behind the destruction you witnessed if you know the importance of the railroads," he said at last. "The War Between the States was the first great conflict in which railroads furnished the chief means of transportation. More than that, railroads were one of the chief causes of the war. The firing on Fort Sumter on April 12, 1861, was simply a climax to a long series of quarrels between North and South over interpretation of the Constitution. The North wanted power in the federal government. The South wanted states' rights. The North wanted the federal government to sponsor railroads. Espousing the Confederate cause from principle and feeling, I entered its army, and President Davis appointed me superintendent of railroads.

"It was an impossible task. The North had twice the miles of railroads and industry and mineral resources. We struggled without supplies. As I traveled about trying to keep trains rolling, I looked through cracked car windows and saw my engines standing cold upon the sidings, their wrought-iron tires worn nearly away. Locomotives breathed like consumptives. Rolling stock screamed for lubricating oil and was given only pig grease.

"You must understand that in early days, railroads were owned by states, counties, or municipal interests and built with different gauges of track. Interference from Richmond was feared as a plot from a competitor, so the doctrine of states' rights created problems.

"I pleaded that the power of regulation be vested in the government. At last Congress acted. President Davis signed my railroad law requiring any carrier to devote its facilities to the support of the army and obliging railroads to adhere to schedules prescribed by the government. Congress passed my law, but when the time came for my reappointment, that was denied.

"By 1863, Richmond was ringing with criticism of Yankees in southern government. I was loyal to the Confederacy, but spoke in sharp phrases that rasped on southern ears. I took on southern life, but I failed to absorb the southern flair for diplomacy and tact. At any rate I returned to Louisiana.

"When our cause was lost, my job and my fortune were swept away. Despair made life seem over."

Bong! Bong! The clock struck eleven, reviving the tremendous man and the tiny girl who had sunk beneath the weight of the past.

"I may remark that I do understand your despair— hatred—fear. But with grit and gumption, anyone can begin again. As I told you at dinner, my offer came to return to Georgia, but stiff negotiations were necessary before I was made president of the Central in 1866.

"The only thing I boast of," he concluded, "is that none of my powers have rusted from disuse. Nothing can defeat you as a person except succumbing to bitterness or hopelessness. Be the best you can be whatever the situation. Keep yourself in high esteem."

"Thank you, sir." Libba rose. "I do appreciate your taking time to tell me this. Good night, Colonel Wad—"

"Wait. Don't ever forget what I've told you. But wait." His stern voice softened. "I do understand that you want to know about your family."

His eyes searched her pale face. "The knowledge could be painful."

She nodded solemnly.

"Do you have any facts?"

"This is my only link."

With trembling fingers, Libba unfastened the chain from around her neck. She removed the turquoise ring. For a long moment she pressed it fearfully against her mouth until a salty taste of blood told her she was biting her tongue.

Her thumb pressed a carved flower. With her hand shaking violently, Libba held out the open ring.

four

The ring looked insignificant in Wadley's massive hand. As he gazed into the glassed compartment, his broad shoulders sagged into an uncustomarily hopeless posture.

"This is all you know of your past?"

Libba's throat worked but no sound emerged. She nodded.

"Well!" He laughed shortly. "The impossible simply takes longer. Let's see what the ring tells us. It is a fine Victorian piece of mourning jewelry. This lock of hair preserved under glass would, most likely, be your mother's."

Libba lifted a black curl and asked, "You think my mother has golden hair?"

"Had, my dear. A mourning ring would have been made for you on the occasion of her death."

"Oh."

"We'll assume, then, that you resemble your father."

Acknowledging his encouragement with a wan smile, Libba said, "There's an inscription."

The lamplight's glow revealed writing on the under-side of the compartment lid: Jonathan Ramsey m. Luther Elizabeth King June 6, 1856.

"You know, then, that these are your parents?"

"Yes, sir. I'm certain of that—and my name."

Snapping the ring shut, Wadley blew his breath against the blue-green stone and polished its gentle luster. His voice was low, musing. "Turquoise is a fashionable gemstone—as fashionable at the moment as hair jewelry. It is a symbol of wealth many people wear; however, I hazard whatever reputation I now have that this particular ring can tell us more. The quality of the gem indicates a fine Persian turquoise. The gold carving and filigree are exquisite."

Endine should be impressed, Libba thought bitterly.

"Yes," Wadley said tersely. "I see a man of wealth and culture in the throes of great grief—perhaps losing a beloved wife in childbirth as so often happens to the frail—having this token of remembrance fashioned for that child in what has long been established as the birthstone for—now, let me see. . . ." He drummed his fingers. "Ah! December."

Wadley reared back with his hands behind his head, pleased with himself. Libba huddled in her high-backed chair, fighting through wisps of long-suppressed memories.

At last, she spoke. "I don't know my birthday. I remember a tiny, white-haired woman, thin yet erect. I called her Nannie." Her words came slowly as though from far away. "She kept saying Savannah would be safe. When we got there, I don't know. My mind goes blank. I seem to see a fort, hear loud, loud guns. I remember smelling smoke. I was so scared. So scared. Crying. She said—Nannie said, 'Now you are six. Too old to cry. You must not cry anymore.' "

Libba felt as though her whole body had filled with tears, as though they must drip from her very fingers and toes.

"Probably Fort McAllister." Wadley's voice, too, had a dead sound. "Major-General Sherman took Savannah and telegraphed a message which reached Lincoln on Christmas Eve of 1864. Savannah citizens will never forget his words: 'I beg to present you as a Christmas gift the city of Savannah.' "

Colonel Wadley sat capping and uncapping a locomotive-shaped, china inkwell. "If we are correct, you would become eighteen some time this December."

They remained for a long time in silence without realizing that Rebecca Wadley stood watching.

"Tcch, Tcch," she said, clucking her tongue. "Enough sad talk. To bed for you, little one. Tomorrow I'll take you to Macon for tea at Mrs. Johnston's. Her social contacts are wide ranging." She put her arm around Libba's thin shoulders and urged her up.

"I hazard that if Jonathan Ramsey still has property along the railroad, I should be able to find out about him," Colonel Wadley said just a shade too heartily.

Libba climbed into the bed thinking, *Three hundred miles of railroad!* Mercifully, she slept but did not dream.

Taking her Sunday gingham from the wardrobe the next day when it was time to dress for the trip into Macon, Libba cried out in dismay at the gravy stain on the crocheted collar. The only other thing she owned was a dark skirt and white shirtwaist. If there were a possibility that she might glean information about her family from Mrs. Johnston, she hated to appear meanly dressed.

With a knock and a simultaneous opening of the door, Endine whirled in with three frocks across her arms. "These bodices are too tight for me," she said, throwing out her chest proudly. "They're big enough for you if you want them."

Sensing contrition beneath the arrogance, Libba accepted graciously. "Thank you. I've never had anything so lovely!" She stroked a gold satin dress and held it against her cheek in childlike wonder at the feel of it as part of her.

Endine's smug smile dropped. "Why don't you wear this street dress? It would be more appropriate. The light blue will bring out your beautiful eyes."

Libba smiled radiantly. "Oh, how can I thank you, Endine? I was afraid I would embarrass you and Miss Rebecca with my shabby—"

Endine laughed. "No one would notice your clothes with that milky skin and those eyes like blue luster saucers. But one does feel more confident when dressed in style." She rubbed a thoughtful finger on her freckled cheek. "If you don't mind hand-me-downs, I have lots more things."

"I *truly* appreciate your generosity."

Endine darted in and out of the room, filling the bureau drawers with cotton stockings, garters, underdrawers, chemises, veils, and gloves. Victorians never showed any skin except that on the face and hands. Dresses in the latest fashion, trimmed with tassels, gimp, fringe, beads, flowers, and bows were hung in the armoire with a dramatic presentation.

"Here is m'lady's breakfast gown, her day gown to go into town, her evening gown for the dinner hour, and her walking gown for the stroll after dinner."

Libba touched the lacy, flounced, white evening gown with hesitant fingers that drew back quickly lest the lovely thing disappear like a froth.

Incredulous that Libba still wore a little girl's corset, Endine laced her tightly into a pear-shaped busk. "You must have a new shape," she said, popping out again, and returning with a horsehair bustle.

After she had donned the corset cover and petticoats, Libba held up her arms as Endine lifted the dress over her head. Smooth, cool, the taffeta slid over her fingers and settled around her. Libba shivered in delight. "Ohhhh," she breathed as she looked over her shoulder in the cheval glass at the tiers of pleats that formed a slight train. She stood very still as Endine wrapped her in an apron of matching blue satin, draping the fullness to accentuate the bustle. Ribbon-bound points floated out behind as Libba strutted about enjoying the sound of the rustling taffeta.

Capturing her hair with a ribbon at the nape of her neck as Endine directed, Libba secured a small blue hat with two long hat pins. The costume was completed by a tiny cape.

"Now you look like a lady going to town. Why don't you rest on the chaise longue while I dress?"

Libba nodded, but she remained standing, gazing into the looking glass after Endine left her. She had never worn this many undergarments at one time. She had never owned this many at one time. She preened, admiring the sophistication of the narrow-skirted silhouette. How did one ever keep up with gloves, fan, and parasol? When she tried to take a deep breath, her corset cinched her waist so tightly that she discovered shy Victorian ladies needed fainting couches, but she was too excited to lie down.

Bouncing down the stairs, she paused at the turning.

Paul gazed up at her with a look she had never received before. She threw back her shoulders and held her head high lest the precariously perched hat betray her and fall off. Slowing her tomboy gait, she drifted toward him with a regal air, aware of the delightful little cape floating behind. For the first time in her life, she basked in the warmth of male admiration. Was she giddy because of the corset stays or because of Paul's roving eyes and bewitching smile?

With a sweeping bow, Paul touched his forehead to the white linen undersleeve falling over her hand and said, "Your servant, m'lady."

Libba giggled as he continued to press her fingers and brush his mustache across her hand in nibbling kisses. Tremors of sensations she had never known fluttered up from deep within her. Excited by the nearness of this vigorous man yet frightened because she could not control the beating of her heart, she tried to pull away.

Paul would not release her. He lifted her hand above her head and twirled her in a pirouette, appraising her appearance from all angles. "Nice!"

"It's Endine's. I. . . ."

Endine had given her a façade of tantalizing womanhood. She swallowed. Much as she longed for love, she knew she was not schooled in the flirtatious handling of a handsome man. How would she calm herself enough to behave sensibly if he came on the excursion with them?

Part of her wanted to rush back upstairs, to don her little girl's corset and old brown calico, to run—

"It suits you perfectly," Paul was saying.

Fanning her lashes back from innocent blue eyes,

Libba looked up at him. He was wearing a workshirt. He had left the collar open, exposing the strong column of his neck, the vein that moved as he smiled. *He is not going.*

"I believe I'll join you. I'm suddenly hungry for afternoon tea."

Startled that he seemed to read her thoughts, Libba jerked her hand away. Trying to take a deep breath past the corset stays, she struggled to regain her composure.

"I can't imagine you holding a tiny teacup in those enormous hands," she said teasingly.

"A long tall glass is more my style," he replied, grinning, "but I do make exceptions, and this—"

"No men allowed," Endine said airily as she clattered down the stairs. With a perfunctory kick in her brother's direction, she moved between them.

Libba's emotions, like the fragmented bits in the kaleidoscope, tumbled, patterning joy, fear, hate, love.

At that moment Colonel Wadley emerged from his study with a carpetbag in his hand, dispelling Paul's aggression as his commanding presence filled the hall.

Wadley already had his mind on a boardroom fight he was anticipating with relish. He hurried the women into the carriage. Taking the reins himself, he clucked to the horses.

The village of Bolingbroke was important because Wadley lived there. Twenty-four trains ran through the community in a twenty-four-hour period. Wood was stacked in readiness by the track. On the pond, a pumper was busily filling the tank with water for the next engine. A whistle blew. Around the railroad yard, old men took out pocket watches and checked to see if the train was on time.

Before he left them in the Macon depot, the colonel drew Libba aside. Promising to inquire about Jonathan Ramsey, he said, "Remember what I told you. Grit and gumption, Libba. Gumption and grit."

She smiled at him courageously, but her smile slipped as their hired carriage swung down Mulberry Street and she saw the boulevard lined with mansions. Macon was a city. Finding the young man to thank him would be impossible.

The carriage stopped before a towering, red-brick Italian Renaissance villa. On either side were ginkgo trees with leaves like sparkling golden fans.

Endine laughed at Libba's astonishment. "Hardly expected to have high tea at an Italianate palazzo, did you? It boasts seven stories, counting the cellar, the two-story cupola, and the top belvedere—it has a secret—" Endine's eyes danced mischievously.

Rebecca interrupted. "When Anne and William Johnston honeymooned in Europe, they brought back furnishings and Italian artisans. We were attending a party to celebrate its completion in the spring of 1861 when we heard that the War of Northern Aggression had begun. It's the last great house of antebellum Georgia. I doubt it will ever be surpassed."

Libba climbed white marble stairs and stood on the marble-floored portico in her borrowed finery, thinking what a long way she had come from the Savannah Female Asylum.

Twelve-foot, arched doors swung open on silver hinges. A white-coated butler admitted them.

Mrs. Johnston, attired in a floating green tea gown,

hurried into the room as though she were at fault for keeping them waiting even a moment.

"My dear Anne," said Rebecca. "I want you to meet my ward, Luther Elizabeth Ramsey."

"I'm delighted you came to tea." Anne Johnston's refined voice wrapped Libba in hospitable warmth. "Do come into the drawing room and we'll get acquainted."

Mrs. Johnston spoke into a silver tube mounted into the wall. They seated themselves around a gilt tea table, and the butler appeared with a mahogany tea cart.

"What kind of tea would you prefer?" Anne Johnston's eyes twinkled. "Rebecca says my Indian souchong smells as if it were meant for men smoking cigars."

Rebecca laughed. "If you still have that pekoe you brought back from London, that would be delightful. I'm not adventuresome enough to change from China tea to the Assam teas."

"You're not adventuresome enough to try green tea!" Anne winked at Libba. "Do you know tea, my dear?" she asked, then hurried to answer her own question to put the girl at ease. "Different kinds all grow on the same plant . The difference comes from the position of the tea leaves on the stem. It's green if it's left unfermented. To become black tea, the leaves are cured."

Her hands moved deftly, taking loose tea from separate, foil-lined tea caddies and sprinkling it into two porcelain teapots. She added water from a steaming kettle.

"Tea is all the same, yet different. A connoisseur can tell by taste the country, altitude, and climate, in which the tea was grown. I rely on Richard Twining and his Golden Lion shop in London's West End where it's been since 1716. He was granted the Royal Warrant by Queen Victoria."

Libba thought her hostess regal, too. She glanced upward at the moldings beautifully carved with a woman's head. Was it Mrs. Johnston? Libba thought not. The carving was not a unique person, but one of many, like she herself.

Libba decided to try the souchong. The thin china teacup rattled and bumped the saucer as Libba shakily started to sip. She realized the others were waiting.

"How do you take it?"

"Well, with lem—" Endine nudged her. There was no lemon, only cream and sugar on the silver tray. "P-p-plain," she stammered. She liked sugar. At the orphanage they followed the Russian manner of using lemon to prevent scurvy. Libba winked a thank you to Endine. When she took a swallow, her mouth drew. No wonder they added milk. The tea was so pungent and malty it was barely drinkable.

The butler presented a tray of tiny sandwiches. "There are cucumber, watercress, smoked salmon, egg salad."

"I'll have egg salad, please." She took a bite. It was spicy, brown, delicious. Everyone else had left their plates on the table. She set hers down and it whacked.

The butler split raisin biscuits. Making sure everyone saw the red sugar rose nestled in clotted cream, he grandly spooned cream onto the biscuits.

From a tray, she took a confection shaped like a swan. The other ladies had made verbal selections and waited for the butler to place their pastries on their plates with tongs.

Oh well, Libba thought. Trying to be nonchalant, she

crunched a swan wing.

"Luther Elizabeth is concerned about tracing her family," Rebecca said in a voice which turned the conversation from polite pleasantries to a more serious note. "Her earliest memories indicate that she was in the path of Sherman's infamous march. Since you know all the best families, we hoped you might help. One great heartache of the late war was the children separated from their families—or orphaned."

"I do understand, dear," said Anne. "Homes have been established all over the South by many of the religious denominations. I have worked with Appleton Church Home for Civil War Orphans. I'll look into any inquiries for lost children, but you must not get your hopes up. We've had little success in reuniting families."

The butler presented a tiered dish of napoleons and eclairs, but Libba's appetite was waning with her hopes.

"Perhaps your mother attended Wesleyan Female College?"

Libba wondered what in her speech and bearing made them assume her background was of equal rank with theirs. Her lack of expertise at the tea table was demonstrating Endine's assessment of her as a nobody. Not trusting her voice, she removed her ring and showed Mrs. Johnston the inscription.

Anne shook her head. "I'm sorry. The date puts her younger than I. I didn't know her. You must reconcile yourself to their loss. Accept the hospitality of the Wadleys—Ah, here is Melrose with our last course. Do have a truffle."

Libba sought comfort in the rich chocolate. She had known this lady would give her no information—just as she had known she would never see the funny young man again. She had no family connections, no past. She must begin right here. . . . She blinked. Unpredictable Endine was deliberately smearing cream on her skirt.

"Ohhh, clumsy me!" Endine said. "May I use your washroom, please, Cousin Anne? Do help me, Libba."

Libba followed, but as they started up the stairs, she hissed, "Why did you do that?"

"There are things I want you to see," Endine said airily as she paused on the landing graced by coffin niches set with large Grecian urns. "Do you know who that is in the stained glass window?"

Libba gaped. Set into the jewel-faceted window was the handsome face of a dark-haired man wearing a white shirt with a daring, open collar. "My goodness! That has to be Lord Byron! How did Mr. Johnston ever let her display that daring picture of such a talked-of romantic man? We weren't even allowed to read his poetry."

Staring at the dark, petulant face and exposed neck, Libba imagined Paul and flushed.

Endine laughed, misunderstanding her blush. "Isn't it scandalous? What with all Lord Byron's love affairs and his tragic death. But Cousin Anne doesn't have to ask anything. She inherited a fortune from her father. She even owns a business."

"Oh, does she run it herself? Is it becoming accepted for a woman to work? I must get a job to support—"

Endine sniffed her freckled nose and flounced up the remaining stairs. "Of course not. It's acceptable for a lady to own a business but certainly not to work! Not out in public!" She grinned conspiratorially. "But forget that. Look at this." She waved her arm at a copper-lined, rosewood tub and a water closet. "They built this house in the late 1850s with hot and cold running water!"

While she dabbed at the cream on her skirt, Endine continued her stream of gossip designed to impress Libba.

"During the war, W.B. Johnston was premier of the Confederate States Treasury. This house held the largest gold and silver depository south of Richmond!"

Uneasiness prickled Libba's neck because Endine's every movement was accompanied by giggling.

"You just want to moon over Lord Byron again," Endine taunted as they returned to the landing. She stopped before the stained glass window and Libba, following her gaze to the picture, was caught offguard by a sudden sharp elbow jabbing her ribs. Libba's shoulder struck the huge porcelain urn in the coffin niche setting it rocking. Terrified lest she break it, Libba clutched air.

Swaying, she stumbled, fell backward. The very wall failed to support her, melted away. She lay flat on her back again. Stunned, she sniffed a penetrating odor. She wondered if her senses were leaving her. Would her nightmares now invade her days? Fighting panic, she sat up. She was alone in a close, doorless room. How had she gotten into this suffocating place?

"Endine. Endeen! Endeeeen!"

five

"Endine! Let me out!" Libba cried. Her prison had a window, but it had *no* door. The odor of cedar came from shelves laden with linens. Was this the rumored gold depository or simply a linen closet? Why a secret room?

How did I get in here? Disoriented, she struggled to remember. She could see no trap door in the ceiling through which she could have fallen. Fuzzily, she recalled an elbow in her ribs. *Endine tricked me into looking at Byron and . . . . Yes! She pushed me against the wall. It moved!*

Calmer now, she examined the wall, found concealed hinges. The panel would neither slide nor push. Suddenly it glided noiselessly inward.

"Endine, you rascal, I oughta—" Her words whooshed in her open mouth.

Wearing stern expressions, Rebecca and Anne stared as the hidden door swung back to reveal the red-faced girl.

Libba stammered, "I . . . I apologize, Mrs. Johnston. I don't know that—I must have leaned—I hope I didn't break. . . ."

Endine cackled. "Libba's moony over poets. She swooned into the niche."

"Someone must have left the catch to the linen closet unfastened," Mrs. Johnston said without her usual smile.

The wall matched the one at the opposite end of the landing. There was no telltale crack, no sign of a catch.

Obviously, Endine knew the secret of the hidden room.

On the homeward trip as the train chugged its way up the hills of Monroe County, Libba laughed with a nonchalance determined to drench Endine's mirth; but resentment at the embarrassment her spiteful friend had caused smoldered like a burning coal beneath her ribs.

Libba awakened at dawn. Still feeling resentful, she cast aside Endine's pretty garments and put on her old clothes. She slipped out into the misty September morning. Flexing her shoulders which ached from the tenseness of holding her feelings in check, she was pleased to be the first one up. She wanted to walk enveloped in fog until her swirling emotions cleared.

A wiry little dog trotted down the path. Behind him followed an old man carrying a bucket. As he came toward her, she saw it was filled with foaming milk, bubbling over, running down the side. Libba nodded, but the man ignored her.

She recoiled as if from a blow. Had her escapade been told? Would even the servants ostracize her?

When his sliding steps came even with her, she sniffed at her inflated sense of importance. She was not worth everyone talking about her, of course. This man was blind.

"Good morning!"

He stopped, sloshing milk. "Morning. Who be you?"

"Libba Ramsey. I thought I was the first one up."

"Heh, heh, heh, you ain't gonna never beat Miss Sarah."

Amazed at the way the terrier was leading, Libba fell into step. "That certainly is a smart dog."

"Heh, heh, heh." He laughed again. "They thought when old Henry went blind, he'd have to give over the milking, but they had another thunk comin'. Old Rags, he teached hisself to take Henry where he needs to go."

In the brick dairy, Sarah Lois greeted Libba warmly. She took the milk, folded a clean cloth over the bucket's lip, and poured an aerating stream over a cornucopia filled with ice in the center of a tin tub.

"Where do you get ice way out here, Miss Sarah Lois?"

The tall woman considered the little face pinched with distress like the puppy she had saved from a drowning. Tenderness softened her plain features. "Why don't you call me 'Auntie' like all the children do?"

"Yes, ma'am!" Libba's face glowed. "Thank you."

"The ice comes on the train once a week. We put it in a croaker sack and bury it in a hole lined with sawdust. Since you're ambitious enough to be up, you may wash this bucket."

Chores finished, they started out. The door to the other half of the building stood open. Kneeling before the steel safe was Paul.

Libba wished she had not let anger at Endine keep her from putting on one of the pretty frocks.

Paul folded money into a leather wallet and flashed a grin at her. "You are an early bird."

Libba smiled, too tongue-tied to talk. *You are certainly not the idle rich I have heard about*, she thought.

"I'm hungry as a bear," he said, leering at her and popping his teeth. "Are you ready for breakfast?"

The boisterous family enjoyed a hearty breakfast before scattering in all directions for various pursuits. After helping with the last task, Libba tucked the small volume of poetry into her pocket and headed outdoors.

The pungency of the black-green boxwoods drew her toward the formal garden. Sentinels of tall thin cypress brought, Auntie had told her, directly from Italy stood watch at the perimeter. Libba stepped through the entrance onto a granite-lined path. Before her descended a panorama of boxwood-bordered terraces. The upper level brimmed with chrysanthemums waving pink, daisy blooms. Rock steps led down each terrace level into— what? Everywhere boxwood concealed and revealed, making the depths unseen, mysterious.

Down below, the surprise lilies beckoned her again. This time she succumbed. Apprehensively at first, she stepped downward, timidly examining each layer.

Suddenly she stepped into a fairyland like an artist's painting of autumn joy. Swamp sunflowers reigned, towering over Libba's head. Artemisia waved its fronds of silver lace. Fat, pink heads of sedum bowed at her feet. And, oh, the asters, tumbling everywhere! She plucked one bright blue blossom and tucked it into her hair. Knowing it matched her eyes, she longed to meet Paul, feared to meet Paul.

As she continued downward, her heedless footsteps pressed thyme and mint, releasing clean, fresh fragrance. In the middle of the garden was a paved circle with granite benches ringing a sculpture of a slender youth. With broad-brimmed hat and sandals adorned with small wings, Hermes paused in his flight over land and sea.

Libba tapped the caduceus in his hand. "Do you bear a message for me?" Liking the Greek messenger's company, she sat on a bench and took out Elizabeth Barrett Browning's book. She read the plaintive lines from the invalid wife to her tender, supportive husband:

> *What can I give thee back, O liberal*
> *And princely giver, who hast brought the gold*
> *And purple of thine heart, unstained, untold,*
> *And laid them on the outside of the wall*
> *For such as I to take or leave withal,*
> *In unexpected largesse? Am I cold,*
> *Ungrateful, that for these most manifold*
> *High gifts, I render nothing back at all?*
> *Not so; not cold,—but very poor instead.*

She thought of her helpmate at the train and winced at her rudeness. He could not have guessed at her vow never to cry. She had treated him with unforgivable coldness.

Would that she could pen a note to him as Mrs. Browning had done to her Robert.

Words flitted through her brain, teased her, vanished behind a worry bush before she could capture them into a line of poetry.

She shook herself. She should go back, inquire if there were other chores. But, the air felt fresh against her cheek. The breeze stilled, then flaunted the leaves, tempting her. The path wound intriguingly downward. She followed.

Now the garden became forest. Ferns and wood's violets nestled in brown leaves that rustled as squirrels scampered to a creek where laughing water leapt over rocks, kissed yearning ferns, dashed heedlessly on.

Click-chug! Click-chug! Click-chug! In the green stillness, the sharp staccato sounded a startling note.
Alarmed, she drew back. The sound ceased. Voices
drifted upstream. Paul! With lightened footsteps, she
picked her way around a bending.

Below a waterfall, several men were working.

"Hello!" Paul called out. "Exploring Auntie's
garden?"

"Yes. It's the most enchanted spot I've ever seen."

"Come see what we're doing. I'm designing a system
to give running water for the house and livestock." He
took her hand to help her over a fallen log.

Trembling with delight at his touch, Libba watched
him adoringly. He showed her how the weight of the
water flowing over a lever clicked the valve shut and the
recoil hurled the water against an inner valve, opening it.

Libba did not understand his explanation of hydrau-
lic machinery. "You must be the smartest man in the
world to make water pump itself with no other source
of energy."

"The principle was discovered in the seventeenth cen-
tury by a Frenchman named Pascal. I've only adapted it.
With a plentiful flow of water and a fall of only a foot and
a half, the ram pump can lift the supply 250 feet," he
explained. "Water is forced into this pipe and up the hill
to a cistern. The water in the holding tank will have
strong pressure from gravity—but come—let me show
you." He pointed the way up the hill.

With clasped hands swinging between them, they
crossed the open meadow. Before them stood the tower
that had aroused Libba's interest, a grand, round column
of brick encompassing the water tank. Architecturally

beautiful, it had a high-arched doorway and, inside, a spiraling staircase.

Libba saw the strength and permanence of this great family symbolized in the brick outbuildings. No make-shifts or simple log structures were here, no simple country people. Dwarfed, Libba dragged back on Paul's hand. She gazed up at the turret—the transported tip of a fairy castle?

Looking at the high round window, she whispered, "I expect to see Rapunzel letting down her hair."

Paul gave a deep-throated laugh. "Umm-huh. Come see." Slipping his arm around her wispy waist, Paul made a show of helping her up the steel spiral.

Tremors of fear tickled Libba's spine as he guided her up the narrow staircase. She should not be here unchaperoned. Her footsteps faltered. She should turn back.

Caught in the winding circle of the stairs, she stopped breathing as he wrapped both arms around her. He brushed his mustache back and forth across her cheek. Suddenly he pressed his mouth upon her innocent lips.

A clattering of boots preceded John's head up the steps. "Paul? Oh, there you are. Hello, Libba. Is Paul showing you Captain Raoul's water system?"

"Yes." Libba could barely recognize her voice over the buzzing in her ears as she drew away. Fearing her face was painted with guilt, she stared out of the fairy-tale window. She had long dreamed of the poetry of a first kiss. Placing a finger to her lips, she could not bring to memory that snatched moment. She felt only embarrassment and fear.

Libba's infatuation, fueled by the fact that Paul left the plantation on business, grew more giddy with each passing day. She spent long hours leaning Rapunzel-like from her window, enjoying feeling sad and singing songs of parted lovers.

Saturday at midmorning, Auntie decided to make sweet potato pies. Removing a key from the ring at her waist, she sent Libba to bring her some brown sugar.

Humming to herself, Libba lifted the key to the door of the creamery. Ajar, it moved.

Paul! He had returned! He was opening the safe, and he merely nodded as she went by him timidly and slid back the top from the brown sugar barrel. The hair on the back of her neck prickled as she stood on tiptoe to scoop sugar into her bowl.

The safe slammed shut. Paul stepped behind her, circled his arm around her, and reached into the barrel.

"The best sugar is this that's stuck around the rim." He pulled off a hunk of the crystallized sugar and popped it into her mouth. Leaning against her, he reached again and took a handful for himself, focusing his dark eyes on her as he crunched.

With candy sweet upon her tongue, she lifted eager lips, knowing his kiss would be as sweet. His mouth came down to meet her lips. His hand stroked her hair, pulled down, forced her head back. His mustache tickled her throat.

Frightened by what was happening, she dropped the bowl into the sugar barrel. He grasped both her wrists. She struggled. "No, Paul. Stop!"

The heavy door creaked, swung open. Libba saw Endine's pulsating freckles and gaping mouth. Behind

her a tousle of gray-streaked hair jerked back in surprise.
A round, boyish face peered with wide, blinking eyes.

Libba snatched the blue bowl from the barrel and
thrust it between her and Paul. Primly she marched out
into the sunlight's glare.

Endine was nearly as flustered as Libba. "This gentleman, uh—came looking for you."

"My name is Daniel Marshall," he said quickly. "I
didn't mean to intrude, but—"

"No, no," Libba stammered. "I'm so glad you . . .
came. I . . . you were so kind, and I was so rude that I've
been. . . ." She clung to the bowl, stared down at it,
suddenly saw it. "Oh! Auntie will be waiting for this.
Please excuse me. I'll be right back."

Without looking at any of them, Libba fled toward the
kitchen. She could hear Paul, self-possessed, the perfect
host making the visitor welcome.

In the dim hall, Libba leaned against the wall until her
breathing became normal. Auntie had grown impatient,
but she excused Libba when the red-faced girl explained
about the kind young man who had come.

When she returned to the yard, Endine and Paul had
led her guest to the scuppernong arbor. They were
strolling beneath it reaching up to pluck the bronze
scuppernongs.

Daniel turned, blinked his eyes. A smile spread over his
candid face infecting Libba.

"However did you find me?"

Daniel wondered how to begin. Why had he been so
foolish as to think himself welcome here? He could
hardly tell her that from the first moment he saw her he
had thought of nothing else. "You know the Chinese—"

He laughed and changed to a tone that poked fun at his own lack of knowledge. "Or is it the Indians? Anyway. They believe that if you save a life, you are responsible for it. So you see. . . ." He shrugged. "I had to find you and be sure you were all right."

Libba met his gaze, and it seemed as if he could see some of her fears receding. What had he witnessed between her and Paul? He was more handsome than any man had a right to be. *He does seem happy to see me now.*

"I'm fine," she said at last. "Be ye Chinese or Indian, I thank you for saving me. It's nice to have a friend!"

"Speaking of Indians," Endine interrupted. "I have a marvelous idea! Why don't you stay for dinner, Mr. Marshall? Then, this afternoon we could all go explore the old Ocmulgee fields and have a picnic!"

"I'd be honored, Miss Endine," Daniel said with a bow. "Perhaps, if we all keep close watch over little Libba here, she won't hurt herself again."

"Now, wait a minute," Libba protested, laughing. "Maybe you've found out too much about me."

When the plantation bell clanged noon, they found that Auntie had already added a plate.

Daniel took hardy helpings. He was famished, but it was difficult to eat this close to Libba. Endine, on his other side, talked steadily.

"You never did say how you traced me," Libba said softly when Endine paused for breath.

"Easy," he replied. "Everyone knows the Wadleys and Great Hill Place. I thought you were part of the family 'til I learned they all have dark eyes and red hair." He gestured down the family table. "No one could forget

those innocent blue eyes of yours. And then I recalled—" His cheeks went slack.

He had remembered her putting her hand over a patch.
If she were also destitute, she might not think little of him
because his fortune vanished in the war.

Willie Wadley, host in his father's absence, spoke into
the sudden silence. "Tell us about yourself, Mr.
Marshall."

"Well, sir." Daniel cleared his throat. "My father was
Morrison Marshall. He was a member of the Macon
Guards. He was killed at Gettysburg."

"I've heard of him," replied Willy. "You may be proud
that he died a hero."

"Thank you, sir. My mother and I still live at Morrison
Hall." He paused. It was unnecessary to explain the
conditions. He had no need to let the Wadleys' wealth
intimidate him. He finished simply, "I teach at Mercer
University."

"Admirable. Admirable," said Willy.

After they demolished the pies, Daniel went out with
the men while the women prepared for the picnic.

Insisting that Libba must be attired in the proper
sportswear, Endine brought her a gray, textured silk
that had a pleated underskirt which allowed freedom in
walking.

"Ohhh! We're going to have such fun!" Endine exclaimed. "You won't believe all the strange things you're
going to see! An excursion to Brown's Mount is
everyone's favorite."

The party included John and Auntie. Libba could
hardly believe the good fortune of a safely chaperoned
outing with Paul and a suitor for Endine.

The jaunty rhythm of the clacking rails played accompaniment to the merriment of the group. The train trip into Macon was all too short. There they piled into carriages and rode across the bridge spanning the Ocmulgee River.

They were in the famous old Ocmulgee fields, the rich low area that had been Indian cropland and ceremonial grounds with beginnings lost in antiquity. They reined the horses beneath a red oak tree and climbed down to show Libba the site of Fort Hawkins, built in 1806 as a trading post with the Creeks.

"During the War Between the States, the Yankees took this old fort and prepared to invade Macon," Daniel said, with his eyes shooting sparks as he launched into his favorite tale. "The enemy battery fired one shot that fell into the heart of the city. I was a lad at the time, and—"

"Oh, Daniel," Libba protested. "Let's don't talk about Yankees. I'd rather hear about Indians."

Daniel's face drooped. Libba turned away.

John was calling her. "Come on, Libba. I'll show you about Indians. Come this way." He pointed to a winding trail.

At the end of the woodland trail, Paul lifted a branch. Stepping out into a clearing, Libba gasped at the strange sight. Straight-sided mounds of earth rose to lofty heights from the level plane of the Macon plateau.

"What?" Libba whispered, staring at the tremendous flattened cones. "How strange! How eerie! The precise form seems to indicate they are man-made, but that seems impossible given their gigantic size! What are they?"

"Indian mounds," replied Paul. "The smaller mounds

were heaped up in honor of the dead," he explained. "But this larger one was the temple mound."

"Who built the mounds?" Libba inquired. "When?"

"No one knows," said Daniel, stepping quickly to her side to capture her attention. He hurried to press his advantage. "All of the Indians in recorded history say the mounds were here when their tribe conquered the area. Even the records of DeSoto in 1540 remarked upon the antiquity."

They showed her where the mound had been cut through when the track was laid for the Central Rail Road in 1842.

"A number of Indian relics were exhumed," Paul said.

"The exciting thing to me," Daniel said, claiming Libba's interest, "was layers used by tribes who perhaps had no knowledge of each other."

"Enough scientific talk," interrupted Endine. "Let's climb up and see the view."

Stronger, more agile, Endine moved ahead of Libba and reached the top. Looking down at the pale girl panting for breath, she called mockingly, "Come on, you can make it to the top. It's magnificent!"

The breeze had died down. The sun had burned away the morning mists. It beamed hot on Libba's back. Raking sticky curls from her perspiring forehead, she wondered how much farther she had to climb. Two hands reached down for her, Paul's strong, brown, beckoning fingers and Daniel's eager, gentle, uplifting palm.

six

Lightheaded, Libba allowed both men to pull her up. Breathing heavily as she reached the flat summit of the Indian mound, which rose fifty feet above the plateau, she wavered, feeling as if she might fall off the top of the world.

"I know it's too wide to fall off—but it feels strange."

"You'll adjust in a minute," Daniel said, soothingly.

"You're hardly on a pinnacle," said Paul, laughing at her. "The top of the mound is one hundred eighty feet north and south and two hundred feet east and west."

"Should we be here—on their burial place? Isn't walking on centuries of graves sacrilege?"

"No," replied Daniel. "This is where they worshipped."

"The sun? Were they trying to reach the sun?"

"No." He smiled at her. "The Muscogee Indians who were here when the British took possession of this country—the British renamed them Creeks because of the small streams or creeks they lived along—anyway, those Indians believed in God, the Great Spirit, the giver and taker away of the breath of life. Their high moral standards prepared for an afterlife in warm and flowery savannas."

"It makes me feel insignificant," whispered Libba.

"Not me," said Endine. "I feel powerful up here. You can see *forever*. Stop being so introspective." She wrinkled her freckled nose at Libba. "Enjoy the view."

Paul grabbed Libba by the shoulders and shoved her toward the sheer drop on the southwest. She shrieked as he pretended to cast her over the side.

"Paul, behave yourself," called Auntie.

"No, look," he said, laughing as Libba hid her face. "Look how far you can see. Can't you imagine an Indian waving his blanket over his signal fire?"

"The great view is from this side," called Daniel, summoning them to where he and Endine stood overlooking the red-stained waters of the Ocmulgee River.

"Above Macon the Ocmulgee is rocky, unnavigable. Macon became a shipping point when steamboating began. It draws trade from cotton fields from all directions."

"But the railroads brought affluence," boasted Paul. "The Central Rail Road arrived here from Savannah in 1843, making Macon the 'queen inland city of the South' at the head of 'the longest railroad in the world built and owned by one company.'"

"I'm impressed," said Libba.

Endine turned her toward the city with its parkways and mansions resembling Greek temples.

"Perfection," agreed Libba. "This scene makes me think of Keats's line, 'A thing of beauty is a joy forever.'"

"Enough tour. Let's eat," interrupted Paul. "Auntie's fried pies may not be a thing of beauty, but they are a joy forever." He smacked his lips.

"Now, what's wrong with the way my pies look?" inquired Auntie tartly.

Joking their way back to the carriages, they rode to Brown's Mount. The road wound gently upward beneath spreading oaks whose cool, damp shade gave welcome relief from the September sun.

They stopped to show Libba the first of many curiosities, a stone wall four feet high and four feet thick.

Paul guided Libba into the ditch behind the wall. "From here the defenders were protected from the shafts of their assailants. These ancient fortifications at one time encircled the entire top of the mount." He underscored his words by circling his arm around her shoulder and squeezing.

Libba smiled up at him coquettishly.

Daniel clenched his teeth. Deftly he stepped to Libba's other side, took her elbow, and left Paul empty-handed. He lifted her back into the carriage, telling her interesting details.

"I wish I could study more and become an enthusiastic teacher, like you," she said.

The carriage rolled around a bend. A deer, drinking from a pond of water lilies, quivered for a timeless moment. Her liquid brown eyes rolled back in fright. She leaped, barely missing the carriage.

In a glade, they spread quilts on the ground and set out crusty fried chicken, huge, fluffy, soda-smelling biscuits, deviled eggs, and Auntie's watermelon rind pickles.

They were reclining and nibbling the pies, bite by ever slower bite, when Daniel said, "I can speak Indian."

Derisive hoots sounded.

"No, really." He jumped up, folded his arms, tucked his chin, and spoke gutturally. *"Tobesofkee Ocmulgee."* Then he sat down closer to Libba "See. Told you."

"Oh, that's not speaking Indian," she said. "You just muttered the name of the creek and the river."

"It's speaking a language if you know what the words

mean. He feigned a hurt expression. His mobile face changed to a triumphant grin. "*Ocmulgee* is Muscogee origin. *Oc* signifies 'water' and *mulgee* means 'bubbling' because of the many springs. *Ocmulgee* means bubbling water. An Indian was crossing the creek in his canoe and lost his provisions. *Tobe* means 'I have lost.' *Sofskee* is a dish prepared with ground corn."

Eyes twinkling, he intoned, "*Tobesofkee Ocmulgee.* Translated: I have spilled my grits in the bubbling water."

Libba laughed and threw a biscuit at Daniel. Happiness was seeping into all of the cold, secret corners of her small, thin body.

John poked Paul. "You're getting fat. Let's play catch."

Paul groaned, but he complied.

Endine and Auntie moved into the shade.

Libba found herself virtually alone with Daniel, not knowing what to say. He began a light conversation, and gradually she realized that talking with Daniel was easy. She did not stammer as she did with most men. His blue eyes rested gently upon her, unlike Paul's darting, probing gaze which excited yet frightened her. As unaccustomed to being in the presence of a friend as she was to being satiated with food, Libba relaxed as she caught Daniel's contagious smile.

"The Wadleys are a wonderful family," he said quietly. "Not affected. Wealth and power don't seem to. . . ." His voice trailed away. He looked directly into her face.

"They're genuinely kind," Libba agreed. "I thought Colonel Wadley was bringing me to be a governess. But Auntie teaches the smaller children and the older ones go into Forsyth." She shrugged. "I guess Mrs. Wadley was really moved with compassion when she found me in the orphanage."

She turned the subject from herself. "Did you say you're a teacher at a university?"

"Yes," Daniel replied. "I'm at Mercer University. There are many fine schools here. Perhaps you could—"

"I doubt I have enough teaching credentials."

"There are two orphans' homes—"

"No!" She shook her black curls vigorously. "I don't have the heart to ever, *ever* return to an orphanage."

Suddenly Libba's story poured forth as she had never shared it with anyone. Daniel listened as she told of her pinch-faced childhood. She had been starved for affection, destitute for clothing, hungry for sufficient food during the terrible Reconstruction era when even the most charitable southerners had nothing to give to the little lost orphans of the war.

"The Wadleys are wonderful," she finished. "But still, I feel I have no place. I'm nobody. Oh, if only I knew the truth!"

Daniel caught her flailing hands in both of his. "A little while ago you quoted Keats. Remember his 'Ode on a Grecian Urn'? ' "Beauty is truth, truth beauty," —that is all/Ye know on earth, and all ye need to know.' You are a beautiful young woman. And, you are beautiful on the inside. That is all the truth you need."

Libba pulled her hands away and hid her face.

Softly Daniel continued, "Don't worry about who your family was. God is your Father. He created you as a very special person. You can do or be anything you strive—"

"That's fine for you to say," Libba flung out bitterly. "You're a hypocrite."

Daniel blanched as if she had slapped him.

"What did you do when Willy asked who you were?" She shook her finger before his blinking eyes. "I remember. You told who and what your father was, where your home was. Last of all, your job. First—first, your family connection—as all good southerners do."

Chagrined, Daniel stared at Libba at a loss for words.

With her hurting heart spreading open before this stranger, Libba turned away. She groped blindly for her shawl. Slanting rays from the brilliant sunset turned dogwood leaves to flickering red flames like her twitching, burning cheeks. A warning of impending night in the quickening breeze chilled the dampness of her forehead as her very marrow seemed chilled.

As if signaled by the plummeting sun, everyone assembled, had one last morsel, packed, and loaded.

Libba turned her back on Daniel and flashed a smiling façade toward Paul. "You worked that down, and you're eating again?" She forced a laugh.

"I'm thirsty," Paul replied, cutting his eyes at her as he took her arm to help her climb back down from the lofty world of the hilltop. "There are four springs issuing from the four faces of Brown's Mount. On the paths leading to the springs, the Indians built stone walls and partially covered walkways. Let's get a drink of the best water you've ever tasted."

"Oh, no!" Auntie intervened. "You won't be taking little Libba looking for hidden passageways. I do declare, Paul Morley, it's men like you who keep a chaperone on her toes."

Paul winked at Libba, but he acquiesced to Auntie.

The interlude ended. They were back in Macon at the

depot. Daniel slipped a folded paper into Libba's hand.

"The Indians believe in circles," he whispered. "They believe nature and men were created by God as brothers. A proverb clings to the Ocmulgee mounds. Chief Seattle wrote, 'All things are connected.' There's a place and time for all things to happen. Maybe someday—" He squeezed her hand.

Libba watched with stinging eyes as he bounded away.

Too keyed-up to sleep, Libba put a flannel wrapper over her gown and crept downstairs. Thirsty, she thought of how Paul would have stolen a kiss had he taken her to the spring.

On the back porch, an oaken bucket of well water was kept on a high shelf. She filled the gourd dipper and drank.

The deep timbre of a voice echoed in the hall. Paul! The gourd shook, dribbling water down the blue robe. His footsteps were coming toward the porch. For him to catch her dressed like this would be scandalous.

"Paul, wait," The slight nasal twang was Auntie's voice.

"Yes ma'am?"

"I must speak with you. You must stop toying with little Libba. You will break her heart!"

Paul laughed lightly. "Now, Auntie, a little flirtation never hurt anyone. I—"

"Exactly! A flirtation to you, but to her—she looks at you like a puppy who has been spanked and is begging for love."

Libba shrank against the porch wall and berated herself for letting her love for Paul show.

"You are the first handsome man who's ever smiled at her. The thrill may soon pass. Worse, she may remain in love with you. Your parents expect you to marry Victoria Landingham."

Paul's easy laughter became a harsh snort. "I'm well familiar with keeping blood blue and combining fortunes to build empires. Just because Victoria is the richest girl in the county—aw, Auntie, you know how affected she is because she's named for the queen. Could I ever satisfy *Queen* Victoria?"

Libba stumbled down the porch steps. Paul's voice penetrated the roaring in her ears.

"Besides, I'm not sure I'm toying with Libba. There's something about our sad-eyed little waif that tugs at my heart. Maybe I'm a little in love with her. Who's to say I wouldn't be happier with Little Miss Nobody?"

Libba began to run. Her feet found blind Henry's path. She ran past the milking barn, out across the meadow.

Wrenching breaths came in great, dry sobs as she fell on the ground and beat her fists. *Little. Little. Little.*

Calmer at last, she lay looking up at the brick arch of the water tower. Only fairy tales ended happily ever after. She must escape again. Tomorrow. She must leave tomorrow. But where could she go? She had nowhere to run.

seven

Libba scowled at her reflection in the mirror. Her eyes were swollen with unshed tears. Her hair stuck out wildly, giving evidence of her night spent tossing about. She attacked her unruly curls angrily, brushing them away from her scalp which seemed to bulge over thoughts wrestling, tumbling, falling over each other. Her body hurt as if their words had been blows.

She must *escape* this house she had hoped would be home.

Paul thought of her as little. Still, he had said he might love her. *But what will happen if he loves me? Would his parents permit our marriage?*

Leaving seemed the only answer. But how?

Daniel. The only person in the world she could truly trust. How could she turn to him? It would be improper. She laughed, imagining the face he would make at that word.

She read the crumpled paper he had slipped to her:

> *Daniel Marshall*
> *Morrison Hall*
> *College Street*
> *Macon, Georgia*
>
> *If you ever need a friend.*

But how could she ask his help? She had lashed out at

him simply because she had allowed him—as no one ever had before—to glimpse inside her soul.

When she trudged down the stairs to breakfast, Auntie greeted her with loving warmth. Libba shuttered her eyes and turned away. Could she trust her? Her face was always set in a smile as enigmatic as the parlor painting of Mona Lisa. She had thought Auntie loved her. That she did not hurt, perhaps, worst of all.

Colonel Wadley had returned and was sitting at the head of the table. His sharp eyes penetrated her defenses. "Libba, after breakfast come into my study."

Fear lodged in her throat, restricting food.

Timidly, Libba knocked on the study door. It pushed open ever so slightly, and she could hear Colonel Wadley dictating a letter to Sarah Lois. She drew back, waiting.

"Father," said Sarah Lois when he ended the letter, "must you travel to Alabama? You are ill."

"I shall have a commissary car fitted up so that I can have privacy. I must look at the Montgomery and Eufaula Railroad. Eufaula has long been an important shipping point for steamboats on the Chattahoochee. Railroads are becoming important there now. I may remark, one day railroads will supplant steamboats, and I must be ready. Ill or not, I must go to Eufaula."

Sarah Lois left frowning. Libba entered fearfully and sank into the chair.

"I have located Jonathan Ramsey's homeplace."

"Ohhh!" Libba sprang to life.

"No. No. It is not good news."

Libba shrank into a hard little knot.

"A Jonathan Ramsey is—or was—the owner of a large

cotton plantation, Magnolia Springs along the Ogeechee River in Bulloch County, Georgia. This must be the same Ramsey. This would have placed you in the vicinity of Savannah. I began searching by backtracking up the railroad from the city."

His terse twang echoed in her ears. Mute, she waited for him to explain in his measured way.

"I'm sorry to tell you this. The land is idle. I may remark, the deeds have never been transferred from Ramsey's name. The property is lying out with taxes unpaid."

"The house?" Libba squeaked hoarsely.

"Burned. Your hatred of Sherman is well founded. Everything was destroyed."

The acrid juices in her mouth could not be swallowed. If her father was alive, how could he have left her with no trace? Was her only legacy a burned-out plantation on which money was owed? As surely as the steamboats were stopped by the rocks above Macon, she could go no farther upstream.

Wadley broke the bitter silence. "This knowledge makes no difference to Mrs. Wadley and me. We knew only your name when we asked you into our home. Mrs. Wadley saw something in you that she wanted to nurture."

Tears rushed to the surface. Libba had never been so near to uncontrollable weeping. She looked at the kindly man and wished she could climb into his lap and cry and be comforted as she had seen his grandchildren do.

Have I repaid your kindness by causing conflict within your family? Libba wondered desperately. *Has Sarah Lois spoken to you about Paul?* John merely had a boyish crush on her. It was a fleeting thing. Was Auntie right? Would her passionate love for Paul also fade? Frightened at the hopelessness of her situation, she knew only one thing to do: run.

"Colonel Wadley, I—" Her voice broke; she tried again. "Your family has been wonderful to me. I . . . hope to remain welcome, but I should. . . . Perhaps, my place is teaching orphans. I understand there are two orphanages in Macon." The words seared her tongue, but she could imagine no alternative. "If you could secure me a position to pay for my living, and . . . and I could still come here to visit. I love your family so much. . . ." Her voice jerked in a snuffling sob.

Wadley considered her for a long time. "If that is what you wish, I will see what I can do."

Overnight the wind had banished September's misty warmth. Crisp air snapped; the sky gleamed clear, bright, heartbreakingly blue. Libba sighed as she took one last look at the dogwood. Yesterday's jolly, red-gold leaves, somber now, were like great drops of blood. With one foot on the carriage step, she gazed longingly back at the house. How she regretted her decision to leave! How could she return to an orphanage after tasting of family and home?

Sarah Lois accompanied her and Colonel Wadley on the silent journey into Macon. By carriage they continued up College Hill and stopped before a tremendous pink brick building. Massive white pillars marched across the front, setting off the recessed center porch. The imposing structure had three stories in each wing, four in the center surmounted by a parapet. This magnificent building could hardly be a charity home. Colonel Wadley must have business here. She drew back in a corner.

Colonel Wadley reached for her hand to help her down. Libba did not stir. "This can't be the orphanage!"

Sarah Lois's plain face broke into a smile at her astonishment. "No. We all agreed our little girl had had enough of sad places. This is Wesleyan Female College. Here you can gain confidence as well as knowledge, polish as well as culture."

"But—surely I'm too old to be a student—even if I had the pedigree to qualify. I'm not good enough to teach."

"Father has thought of everything." Auntie patted her.

In gentle tones reserved for his tow-headed grandchildren, he explained, "My good friend, the Reverend Capers Bass, who is president, offered the perfect solution. He found a vacancy in the preparatory department. You see, the young ladies come here from over several states, and they are unevenly prepared. Some must be brought up to a common level of performance before they begin the college classes. This is especially true of the group who grew up during the war when so many of the British governesses fled from the plantation schools to return to safety in England."

"I suggested," interposed Auntie, "that you might enjoy teaching the course in orthography and English grammar. I know you love poetry, and your records from Savannah indicated. . . ."

Stunned, Libba followed through an iron fence, climbed the stairs, and stepped reverently through the door into the hushed and solemn halls.

Libba could scarcely believe that she was in the "Mother of Female colleges," the first in the entire world to grant the same honors, degrees, and licenses to women as those conferred on men. Her hands were clammy as she curtsied before President Bass. His bald pate shone in the flickering gaslight, and his white mustache and goatee worked up and down as he surveyed her assessingly. Libba was afraid to breathe.

"Welcome to Wesleyan, my dear. Colonel Wadley assures me you will fit well into our program."

"Thank you, sir." Libba curtsied again.

"As a favor to Colonel Wadley," Bass continued, "you will be allowed to audit some of the post graduate courses of Shakespeare, Dickens, Thackery—when you have no duties."

"Thank you, sir!" Her enthusiasm overcame her fear.

Libba followed Auntie down a long, dim hallway to a door marked: Housemother, Miss Cornelia Burt.

Before the tall, handsome woman's penetrating gaze, Libba felt that she was shrinking like Alice. Miss Burt briefed her on the statutes of the college, internal regulations, and the strict regimen.

Summoning a willowy woman, Miss Clifford Cotton, to show Libba to her quarters, Miss Burt laughed.

"I declare, Miss Ramsey, I shall have difficulty distinguishing you from your pupils, you are so small."

Sarah Lois accompanied Libba to the large room she was to share .

Clifford Cotton went at once to the chandelier in the middle of the room. Producing a matchbox, she lifted the chimney and turned up the wick. "You see the trick is to strike your match and light the gas without smoking up the chimney," she said, laughing, "like I just did. Now, I'll leave you to your goodbyes."

Sarah Lois put her arm around Libba's unforgiving shoulders. "You must write to me. If you're not happy here, let me know immediately! Always remember, I am your friend."

Libba's thoughts tumbled. Was Auntie her friend? Or were they separating her from Paul?

Throughout the long dark night, the question nagged. The massive iron fence locked her away from Paul, away from the world, less rigidly than the rules.

Regulations allowed no visiting on the Sabbath. Only lady visitors and near relatives were permitted during the week at such hours as did not conflict with college duties. Gentlemen friends were never allowed to call. Even correspondence with young men was forbidden.

Special permission of the president was required for any student to visit outside college. Homesick for a home that was not really hers, Libba lay thinking of the shining halls of Great Hill Place ringing with laughter. In that wonderful home, one could be surrounded by love or could be alone. Three other teachers slept in this lofty-ceilinged room. She had reveled in having her own bedroom for such a short time. Why had she panicked and fled?

Gradually Libba began to feel more at home. She had no worry about her wardrobe. Rules interdicted the use of jewelry and required simplicity of dress.

The bell rang each day at sunrise summoning them to the chapel for prayer. They were expected to study until breakfast and then have recreation until nine o'clock when the bell rang for morning prayer which preceded recitations. It was a choice thing to ring the bell on the front porch. They went, two girls at a turn, the only time they were let out in public.

In the dining hall, all ate at the same tables. Food was plain, healthful fare with no rich condiments such as meats and cakes. Libba let her mouth remember the taste of cream as Auntie dolloped it on her oatmeal . . . of brown sugar . . . of—No. She must not let herself dream of the candied brown sugar from the barrel, the sweetness of Paul's lips upon hers.

There was little time for daydreams. As busy days passed, Libba worried less about who she had been and wondered more about who she might become if she truly strove. Taking pleasure in helping young pupils, she also learned.

Late one afternoon when Libba was immersed in reading Wordsworth, a tap sounded at her door.

"Miss Ramsey," said Miss Cotton with an enigmatic smile, "you have a caller in the parlor. Your brother."

eight

"You didn't say goodbye," Paul said, holding out his hand.

Libba skimmed across the parlor with her feet barely touching the floor.

"Paul! I—" Her voice echoed—too animated to be greeting a brother. Red spots of guilt quivered in her cheeks.

"How is the family?" she asked loudly. "Auntie? Miss Rebecca?" Covertly she watched the huge Chippendale mirror until Miss Cotton left. "You left first—without goodbye," she said, bristling.

"That's different." Paul frowned. "I had to work."

Around them the hum of voices ceased. Down the long parlor, arranged with chairs grouped around oil portraits, families stopped their visiting to stare.

Libba pointed him to a Sheraton sofa slightly secluded by a potted palm.

"Why did you leave? Did I really frighten you on the Indian Mound? I was only playing. . . ."

Libba fanned back her lashes, and her throat pulsed as she questioned herself. Was he only playing at love? She could not ask about Victoria.

"Paul, I—" Her voice squeaked. Angry at herself, she whispered huskily, "Has it occurred to you that Colonel Wadley sent you on business to keep you away from me?"

Surprised, Paul snorted a rueful laugh. "Maybe. That

doesn't matter. They offered you a home and they meant it. Come back! You know I'm attracted to you, and I know you are to me." He smirked and devoured her with his eyes.

Longing for his touch, Libba was glad for the chaperones. She might not have had the strength for refusal.

"I can't come back now," she whispered. "Later. Maybe. Your family is wonderful, but . . . I'm too rough a stone among all those jewels."

"You have a delicate beauty. Auntie could polish you to whatever luster——"

"I have no dowry at all!"

Paul opened his mouth, closed it. After an uncomfortable silence, he said, "We need time to know each other."

"Yes. I need time to learn—to grow."

His voice rose. "We can't get to know each other in this . . . this nunnery."

"Shhh. It's not that bad. You're here aren't you?"

"But not for long."

It was sunset. Someone appeared to light the gaslights, signaling the end of the visitation. Parents were kissing their daughters goodbye. Paul's handsome face clouded with a bad-tempered scowl.

Suddenly strong, wrapped in Miss Burt's protective rules, Libba could get to know Paul without the frightening whirl of physical excitement scattering her brains. Standing tall, she extended her hand in a grand gesture of farewell that would have done Miss Burt credit.

"Do come again, *Brother*. Tell the family that in this wonderful atmosphere I'm learning to appreciate things of worth and beauty." She laughed. "Did you notice I even descend a staircase properly?"

"I liked the tomboy tumbling down the stairs," Paul grumbled. "Is it true you can't even come home for Christmas?"

Her resolve shook at the thought of a real Christmas at Great Hill Place. Wavering, she reached toward him.

The doors were opening, closing. Paul was gone.

On Sundays Libba's duty was to escort rows of girls marching en masse down the hill to church. Small and innocent as a student, she did little to deter the Mercer boys. They pranced alongside, trying to speak to the Wesleyannes.

In the darkened sanctuary of the old church, Libba sat centered amid her pupils.

The organ's solemn strains indicated heads should bow in prayer, but a scuffling in the pew behind the girls pricked Libba's ears. A hoarse whisper cajoled the Mercer boys to exchange seats. Each in turn grunted refusal. She peeped back.

Daniel, perched at the end of the pew. Rolling his eyes, he pulled his lips over his teeth, forcing Libba into a fit of coughing to cover her laughter.

Being teacher-chaperone for a solemn occasion made it funnier. Giggles escaped. Swallowing her laughter, Libba hiccuped. Miss Burt leaned over and frowned.

Folding her hands as if in prayer, Libba pinched her nose and tried to concentrate on the pastor as he intoned, "Judge not, and ye shall not be judged; condemn not, and ye shall not be condemned; forgive, and ye shall be forgiven."

Suddenly sober, Libba remembered all of the things she could not forgive and merely wanted to forget.

When worship ended, Miss Burt with strength of character no one dared challenge, stationed herself to block the pew. Motioning for girls to file out, she instructed Libba, "Keep the girls moving smartly. The rules of the trustees allow no fraternizing with Mercer boys."

Staunchly remaining, she greeted friends, keeping the boys chafing.

Libba glimpsed Daniel's bouncing head, but saw him no more. Throughout the long, quiet Sabbath, she thought of Daniel and giggled.

The next Sunday as Libba led her girls through the iron gates, she could feel their anticipation. Everyone sensed Daniel liked the challenge of the iron-clad rules. A gaggle of boys waiting beneath the trees across College Street swooped down upon them, matching their marching steps. Strutting like a gander, Daniel tipped a stylish, round hat.

Libba nodded curtly. Holding her chin straight ahead, she cut her eyes at him. His normal attire, clean but rumpled with mismatched colors and missing buttons, was replaced by a new gray jacket that swung open to reveal a double-breasted, plaid waistcoat strung with a gold watch chain.

Eyes darting mischievously, mouth twitching, he started to speak, but she cut him short.

"Daniel Marshall, you'll get me thrown out of school!"

With a droll, contrite expression, he doubled the pace of the girls and marched smartly ahead. Tipping his hat to each row in turn, he descended around the curve and disappeared.

Regretting her curtness, Libba reckoned without Daniel's determination, Mercer boys waited in the church yard. Deftly they took the pew behind the girls. With scuffling and mock refusals to exchange seats, Daniel negotiated one place at a time. At last behind Libba, he warmed her back with his eyes.

Standing for a hymn, Daniel dropped a paper over her shoulder. Unfolding it surreptitiously inside the hymn book, she read, "Forgive this humble hypocrite."

She nodded.

"I must see you," he whispered, breath against her hair before she could sit.

Libba whispered back, "Rules."

The watchful Miss Burt circumvented further contact.

On Tuesday a letter arrived, wrinkled, bearing an ink blot; it could only be from Daniel.

Miss Burt had said correspondence with young men was forbidden, but they never inspected the pupils' letters.

Teachers' letters either, I hope, Libba giggled guiltily and scurried to her room.

She felt Daniel's energy bouncing around her as she read his opening lines, "I'm happy to think of you living and learning in the romantic atmosphere of Wesleyan." She laughed. Daniel must know this to be the most carefully chaperoned place in the world. She had locked herself away from romance. A thought echoed: "Love always finds a way."

She savored his long, warm letter. He told of the romance of his mother's cousin, Mary Day, and Sidney Lanier who were among the refugees who boarded at Wesleyan during the bitter months after Macon was surrendered to the Yankees.

> *He is poet, novelist, teacher, and musician par excellence. I hope to introduce you to them. You share another kinship with him because, like you, he bears the scars of the war with great courage.*

Libba sat reading the poems he had included. Strengthened, encouraged, she took hope that Daniel counted her a friend and thought her worthy to meet so great a man as Lanier.

A few days later, another letter came, smooth, clean, bearing the Great Hill crest. Paul! She ripped it open.

Rebecca's handwriting. She clapped her hand over her mouth to smother a shriek as she read the chatty letter about the engagement party she and Mrs. Landingham were planning for Victoria and Paul.

Clutching her shawl about her shaking shoulders, Libba ran down the stairs to the basement. Like a caged animal, she stalked up and down the dark corridors between the practice cubicles. Sawing violins, scaling voices, and jangling pianos pelted her raw nerves. How many heartbroken sobs had been concealed here? How many ghostly girls still practiced their lessons in this hall, wringing their hands? In this cacophany of music, would anyone notice if she screamed?

After an endless night, daylight came. The thought

remained: *Couldn't Paul care enough for me to wait?*

Numbly, Libba stumbled through her day. That afternoon, a pupil came to tell her there was a lady waiting in the parlor. She stared at the calling card unable to comprehend what her eyes read: Mrs. Daniel Morrison Marshall.

nine

Daniel's wife? Can he be married? Am I so starved for affection that I misread the simple kindness he offered?

Libba could think of no way to escape the interview. Blindly, she descended the stairs and peeped into the parlor.

A wisp of a woman glimpsed Libba and smiled. She moved across the room with her back ramrod straight, her chin up, and her head held as if her snow white hair were a crown. Extending both black-gloved hands, palms upward, she said, "You must be Libba."

"Yes, ma'am." Libba's knees bent, and she prepared to curtsy, but she felt engulfed by the woman's graciousness, and, instead, placed her hands on the outstretched palms. The fragile-looking woman gave her fingers a warm squeeze.

If I could be that beautiful with age, I wouldn't mind growing old, Libba thought, noting the older woman's tissuelike skin, aristocratic Roman nose, and fine, high cheekbones.

"I'm Dorothea Marshall," she said. "My son asked me to make you welcome."

"Thank you." Libba sighed. How foolish she had been to let anxiety confuse her into thinking this would be Daniel's wife!

They sat down on a pair of corset-backed chairs positioned for a tête-à-tête.

"I'm glad Daniel asked me to come." Mrs. Marshall's

eyes sparkled with fun. Her lower lip pressed ever so slightly on her upper teeth as if to suppress ripples of laughter. "I wanted to see the girl who got him to buy new clothes. Now my Morrison. . . ."

While she chattered about her husband as if he had only momentarily left the room, Libba relaxed and appraised her. Although the pert little hat perched at an angle over her forehead was fashionable, her black dress was rusty, and the gored skirt and bustle had evidently been refashioned from an old, prewar hoop skirt.

The interesting, vital woman drew Libba into a lively exchange, and when her call was over, Libba felt that she had found a friend.

But in the darkness of the night, loneliness blanketed her cot. She dreamed of Paul waiting just beyond reach. Achingly awake, she promised that she would never again expose herself to the hurt of falling in love. Worthlessness overwhelmed her.

When the invitation to Paul's engagement party arrived, Miss Cotton watched Libba thrust it away as if it burned her fingers. Confessing her troubles to the sympathetic woman, Libba finished by saying, "How can I *not* go when they have been so kind?"

"Don't worry," said Miss Cotton. "I'm certain Miss Burt will say that the rules of the trustees forbid getting out of school for engagement parties."

"How could the trustees have thought of so many rules?"

"Don't you know? There are no rules for students in the trustees' minutes. Whenever a girl is tempted by something she should not do, Miss Burt makes up a rule on the spot."

Libba laughed. Relieved, she hurried to her duty of supervising day students in the study room. Unable to free her mind of Paul, she was daydreaming over a stack of papers that needed grading when a student timidly interrupted her.

"Your brother is here."

Dumbfounded, Libba looked at the calling card—actually a scrap of paper—with the scrawled initials, "P.M."

Libba upset her bottle of ink. Spreading black stains inched over the papers, obliterating everything.

"Here, I'll clean it up," the girl offered. "You must go." She whispered, "It's your young man."

My young man! Libba dabbed at the ink. *Oh, Paul! Do you really love me after all?*

Forgetting everything, she tumbled down the stairs. Silhouetted against the glow from the fireplace, a tousled, gray-streaked head bobbed back and forth in rhythm to a tune he was humming while he waited. Drawing back into a shadow, Libba pulled the scrap of paper from her pocket. The hoped-for *P* was a *D* with an inky tail.

Forgetting how relieved she had been that Mrs. Marshall was Daniel's mother, not his wife, she now felt exasperated.

"Daniel! You'll get us both in trouble," she reprimanded. "They'll know you're not my brother."

"Neither is Paul."

"How—"

"Oh, I have my ways." His eyebrows went up at the bridge of his nose making a mournful expression. Then he relaxed his features and showed his white teeth in a grin that made him handsome. "Anyway, I had to see you.

Mama said you looked unhappy. We Indians have our responsibilities, you know."

Libba laughed in spite of herself, but the painful lump at the base of her throat refused to dislodge. She could not swallow her disappointment that this was not Paul.

Huddled in a cold little lump, she looked at her clenched hands while Daniel chattered. He sat on the edge of the seat with his vibrant body turned so that he could face her. Ducking his head, Daniel sought her downcast eyes.

Momentarily, she lifted her gaze to meet his. Tenderness, flowing over her, begged to warm her very soul. She caught a tremulous breath and retreated behind thick lashes.

Daniel was leaving. She held out her hand, mumbled goodbye. Trudging up the stairs, she rubbed her aching head and wondered dully what he had said, what she had replied. His vulnerable face swam before her eyes, but she willed it away. She wallowed in the misery of Paul's conversation with Sarah Lois. She pictured a scene where she made her presence known to them and flung out bitter, unforgiving words. All night long, resentment festered.

A few days later as Libba entered the dining hall, President Bass stopped her.

"I have a request for your presence, Miss Ramsey. Mrs. Dorothea Marshall has petitioned a special privilege that you be allowed to attend luncheon with her tomorrow. Her servant will call for you."

"Yes, sir. Thank you, sir."

The old gentleman gave her a courtly bow. "Do accord me the honor of joining me at my table this evening."

Libba's reply came out a swallowed squeak. Students

always sat with a teacher at the head of each table because dining ranked as one of the fine arts, but Libba had never sat with an eminent professor. In a society with no traditional aristocracy, manners delineated class and status. Libba was struggling to learn, but she wished she had more time before coming under President Bass's scrutiny.

President Bass explained that Mrs. Marshall's father had been one of Wesleyan's Trustees; she was denied nothing.

Libba watched as he selected a pointed orange spoon from the array of silver and dipped it into an orange. Trying to dip out the fruit without upsetting the footed orange cup, Libba half-listened to the conversation.

"Did anyone read about the steamboat race on the Chattahoochee?" President Bass asked.

"How is that possible?" asked one of the professors. "It's too narrow a river for two boats to race side by side."

"It's a race against time. The *Columbus Enquirer* stated that the *Mignone Wingate* left the Columbus docks at 8:00 a.m. November 3, to rendezvous with a Liverpool-bound ship in Appalachicola Bay at dawn on the fifth."

"That's entirely too fast!" One of the ladies spoke up indignantly. "Speed is dangerous on a river with so many sandbars and rocks! The Chattahoochee is well named the longest graveyard in the state of Georgia."

"It's hard to believe a well-known captain like Harrison Wingate would attempt anything so foolhardy."

"Still, steamboats must begin to keep schedules and make better time or the railroads will put them out of business," said President Bass, pulling his goatee thoughtfully.

"The pilot is an inexperienced young whippersnapper named Foy Edwards," someone volunteered. "The engineer was in the navy, though. Jonathan. . . . What's his name? One of the men injured when the gunboat *Chattahoochee* exploded. . . ."

Libba had been watching carefully as the orange cups were removed and everyone wiped their fingers on doilies, small, fringed napkins used to protect the dinner napkins from fruit stains. She wiped her hands. The race did not concern her.

Libba dressed carefully, excited at the prospect of luncheon with Daniel's mother. Would *he* be there?

A servant called for her. They walked up College Street to a templelike, white house. Libba stared in amazement. Thick, round columns towering to the flat, balustraded roof, marched eight strong across the front porch. Mrs. Marshall stood waiting. She clasped Libba's hand in both of hers.

"You like my house?" She smiled at Libba's astonishment. "When Morrison was building it for me as a bride thirty years ago, I casually mentioned that I'd always dreamed of a house with white columns." She grinned impishly. "I really didn't dream he'd grant my whim. This was one of the first Greek Revival houses in the area."

"It's magnificent!"

Libba's exalted feeling continued as she stepped into the spacious entrance hall. People filled the entertaining rooms to her disappointment. She was part of a crowd—a crowd which did not include Daniel.

Uncomprehendingly acknowledging introductions, Libba allowed herself to be seated at the place of honor by her hostess's right hand. Delicate bone china, gleaming coin-silver flatwear, and a dozen centerpieces of colorful fruit in cut glass compotes arrayed the long table.

The butler served a multicoursed meal of elegant food enhanced by delicate French sauces.

"Libba, dear," Mrs. Marshall said as she lifted a whole roast squab to her plate. "Daniel tells me you're interested in poetry."

"Yes, ma'am." Libba struggled to use the serving spoon and fork in the same way. "And he tells me you are related to Sidney Lanier. His words make you see and hear his images. They seem to sing."

Mrs. Marshall's smile was a gift of making everyone feel happy in her presence. Libba thought, *She possesses the perception and humor I so love in Daniel.*

Dessert was savored slowly. Finger bowls like blue lotus buds were set before the guests. Libba rubbed her fingertips on the floating orange leaf and dried them on the doily. With compliments on the meal, everyone rose.

While her hostess mingled a moment, Libba stood in a corner trying to take deep breaths against her corset stays. The richness of the food and the opulence of the setting contradicted the mother and son's personal attire. Suddenly Libba saw details she had not noticed: the table linens were discreetly patched; the upholstery was split on several chairs; the paint was scrubbed thin. When Mrs. Marshall spoke close by her elbow, she jumped.

"You're too pale, my dear. Let's take a constitutional."

"Oh, I couldn't take you away from your guests!"

Mrs. Marshall studied Libba for a long moment. "They are quite at home. You didn't know? They are boarders."

Libba looked at her incredulously.

"Paying guests. Since the war, one does what one must." Setting a brisk pace through streets lined with sun-

burnished red oaks and hickories glittering to pure gold,
Mrs. Marshall told how her husband's fortune had been
swept away by war. To save Morrison Hall she had taken
paying guests, many of whom had refugeed to Macon
when Sherman burned their plantations.

Bitterly, Libba related her own tale of Sherman's ad-
vancing army and the terror of her flight.

Mrs. Marshall bit her lips and murmured unintelligible
sounds. She could share Libba's pain, but could she ease
it?

Their heels clicked as they walked swiftly, exorcising
their passion.

"How was Sherman generous enough to spare
Macon?"

"Hardly that!" Mrs. Marshall snorted a laugh. "We
battled for our town. Macon was filled with six thousand
disabled troops crowding hospitals—a number equal to the
population of women and children. We escaped a raid until
the last summer of the war. I was separated from Daniel
when the shelling started, and I was frantic."

Daniel! Libba's heart leaped. Suddenly she wanted to
hear his mother tell about his childhood.

"Our protectors were a company of aged gentlemen, the
Silver Greys, plus hospital convalescents, and so on. The
enemy placed a battery on the east side of the river." She
gestured. "Near the Indian Mounds."

Libba nodded.

"I was working with the Ladies Soldiers' Relief Society.
Daniel was coming along here. He was ten. A cute little
freckle-faced lad. Wide-eyed. Curious."

Libba smiled at the image.

"He and some other children had been helping pack

cartridges. Suddenly a shot from Stoneman's artillery fell right here on Mulberry Street. Daniel and six-year-old William Sims Payne were playing on the sidewalk when a cannonball struck the sand. It bounced, went up through that column, entered the parlor of Judge Holt's house, and landed unexploded in the hall." She laughed. "After the enemy was routed, Mrs. Holt presented the cannonball to the Macon Volunteers."

"But how did you hold them off with no troops?"

"A battalion of Tennesseans, who were heading toward the battle for Atlanta, passed here in time to join Findlay's Georgia Reserves. They spread so wide and yelled so loud that the enemy thought there was an army and retreated."

"And Daniel. Was he hurt when the cannonball fell?"

"No." Mrs. Marshall's eyes crinkled and she pressed her lower lip up on her upper teeth, then burst into laughter. "But you should have seen him telling the tale."

Libba felt a pang of remorse. She enjoyed the animated way Daniel related stories, but she had rudely stopped him at Fort Hawkins when he had tried to tell her this story.

They reached the gates of Rose Hill Cemetery. Mrs. Marshall showed her rows of markers for Confederate dead and told how the ladies defied bayonet rule by placing flowers on the graves with Federal officers watching them.

"We had a true Memorial Day after the troops had been removed. Sidney Lanier made the address."

Libba sensed the scrutiny of her gaze.

"The bitterness of the times did not tarnish dear Sidney's soul even though he had been in Yankee prison. He said to bear our load of wrong and injury with the tranquil dignity that becomes those who would be great in misfortune. I remember his exact words: '... Today we are here for love and not for hate. Today we are here for harmony and not for discord. Today we are risen immeasurably above all vengeance. Today, standing upon the serene heights of forgiveness, our souls choir together the enchanting music of harmonious Christian civilization.' "

They sat in silence. Gradually Libba's numbness tingled into realization. Daniel had shared with his mother how hatred of Sherman and bitterness toward her father strangled her. She blinked back tears.

"Forgiveness is a freeing thing. Unforgiveness eats at the soul until it shrinks away instead of growing. Only as we forgive, can we feel the cleansing of God's forgiveness."

Seeing the caring face of this sensitive woman so like her son, Libba thought, *Daniel must love me if he has taken my problems to his mother.*

Paul's virility had ignited girlish fantasies, enflamed youthful passions, made her spurn Daniel's tender, infinitely caring advances. When last he called, she had coldly turned him away. Could he forgive her?

With heaviness of soul, she thought, *I have been blind, far more blind than poor old Henry!*

ten

Clapping hands, stamping feet, cheering male voices erupted in solemn Pierce Chapel as the Mercer boys applauded the Wesleyan girls' Christmas program. Libba faced the stage, but her smile flickered. After weeks of seeing him only from afar, she was in the same room with him.

It was over. Libba could turn, free her radiant smile to cross the aisle. There with his students sat Daniel.

He mouthed unmistakably, "I love you."

Not caring if her pupils had seen, Libba accompanied them into the dining hall, secure, knowing Daniel would seek her.

The girls knew all. She had become as foolish as they, leaning out of the third story window to watch through falling leaves for glimpses of Daniel. Often he waited across the street eager to return her wave. Afraid he would break the rule by coming to visit, she felt deflated that he did not. Once, on a moonlit winter night, the giggling girls were drawn to the window by the plinking of banjos, the strumming of guitars. Libba leaned far out, not wanting to miss a word of Daniel's serenade.

Boldly she had written to him begging forgiveness for her rudeness. No need to apologize, he said. Of course, he understood. His daily letters were warm, funny, yet tender. Their friendship had blossomed through their correspondence, and now, here he was threading his way across the crowded room.

"Mr. Marshall," Libba said, formally extending her hand. "How nice of you to bring a group to our program."

Correctly, Daniel clicked his heels and bowed before her. Lifting her hand to his lips, he kissed it warmly. "An excellent recital, Miss Ramsey. I apologize for the overzealousness of my men." He was still holding her fingertips. Before he released her, he bent again. Covertly, he pressed his lips against her palm.

Libba nodded mutely, cupping her hand to her cheek, knowing she would never forget the moment of that kiss.

Daniel found a secluded corner.

With their heads inclined toward each other, their eyes meeting over punch cups, they needed no other food. Voices flowed around them like melodies plucked from violins. They stood at the center of the sound sharing a delicious silence.

All too soon he was gone. She was back in her room wondering when she would see him again. She had promised herself after her bitter-sweet pain from loving Paul that she would shut up her heart. She and Daniel would only be friends. Now, as if seeing him for the first time, she knew. He was rescuer-friend no longer. She had fallen in love with Daniel.

Christmas was two days of quiet worship before the girls returned to classes. Then, startling news swept through the dormitory. Smallpox!

With a girl in the infirmary diagnosed, an epidemic threatened. School was dismissed for a fortnight.

Sarah Lois came to get Libba, and she was once again enveloped in the warmth of home.

The next day, Daniel arrived with plans carefully laid.

He had brought Zachary Jones whom he introduced to Endine. Patting her mimosa hair, Endine took Zachary off down the stone steps of Auntie's garden, already embroiled in debate.

Blissfully alone, suddenly shy, Daniel and Libba descended slowly.

He whispered, "I've read and reread every word you've written to me. Between the lines I suspect the soul of a poet—if you'd but open your heart and let your words flow from within."

Libba shook her head. "I could never be good enough to write poetry. Sometimes, I think of a line, but I never have the courage to write it. Someone might see—and laugh."

"I wouldn't laugh. *With* you, of course. But never *at* you."

Libba memorized Daniel's honest face. She knew there was no place in his soul for derision. Understanding and tenderness flowed from his smile, wrapped round her.

They paused in their descent and turned aside onto a terrace devoted to winter beautiful plants. Pristine white narcissus bloomed. Daniel snapped off a stem of the delicate, clustered blossoms. Solemnly, he presented it to Libba as though it represented great worth. Accepting it in kind, she buried her face in the fragrance.

Daniel gently put his arms around Libba. Twining her hands about his neck, standing on tiptoe, she lifted her yearning lips.

"My darling little Libba, I love you. I want to take care of you. I. . . ." He nuzzled her cloud of black hair, brushed her cheek, kissed her.

Wondrous at the flood of long-pent emotions his lips conveyed, Libba joyfully returned his kiss.

They lingered as long as they dared, vowing never to forget this moment of beauty.

Rejoining the others at the pagodalike shelter over the well, they laughed and drank of the fresh, cold water. Nothing in Libba's life had ever tasted so sweet.

Daniel looked at Zachary, lifting the corners of his mobile eyebrows into question marks. Receiving an eager nod, he cleared his throat.

"Ahem! Ladies, I have the pleasure to announce that we are here on an important mission." He made a fist-trumpet. "Ta-toot-ta-too! We wish to formally invite you to our neighborhood New Year's Eve ball. We offer ourselves as your humble escorts."

"Ohhh," Endine squealed. "That sounds like fun!"

"A . . . ball? What would I wear? Oh, I couldn't. Where will it be? Who . . . ?"

"Oh, Libba, don't be so skittish. I've lots of gowns. Of course, you could."

Daniel panicked, floundered, "I want to show you to our friends. It's one of the oldest houses in town. Belonged to a cotton farmer named Joseph Bond. Now his daughter, Mary Lockett—but never mind, Mother will be there to welcome you."

"Shouldn't we ask someone's permission?"

"We'll ask Auntie."

Sarah Lois assured Libba that attending this ball should not endanger her position at Wesleyan's academy. She insisted that she wanted to buy Libba a ball gown all her own.

With their invitation accepted, the gentlemen left amid a great deal of jollity. In the marvelous privacy of her room, Libba pressed her narcissus between the pages of a book.

She'd keep it forever, but she needed no remembrance. She would never forget Daniel's first kiss.

They had decided upon blue to match Libba's eyes. After a great deal of nipping to make the dress drape gracefully over Libba's fragile figure, Sarah Lois declared the ball gown ready.

Libba stood looking in the cheval glass. Her eyes illuminated her delicate face as she stroked the lustrous satin. The back cascaded from her tiny waist into a short train bursting with intricate puffs captured here and there by fluttering bows. *Can I manage all of this on the dance floor? Dare I trust Endine's waltz instructions?*

Carefully she placed the turquoise ring on top of the elbow length, white kid gloves. *In so large a gathering might someone notice it and know who I am?*

Endine's mature figure was encased in apricot satin making an asset of her hair. She took charge of making the foursome merry, and all went well until they reached Macon.

The carriage ascended a hill toward a magnificent site overlooking the city.

Libba's eyes widened in fear. "Daniel!" she exclaimed. "You said a cotton farmer. A party at your neighbor's old house! This looks like we're climbing the Acropolis! Is that the Parthenon?"

Endine laughed. "What did you expect? For all his acting the buffoon, Daniel is *somebody*."

"Yes, but—no, I. . . . Nothing so grand as this!"

Brilliantly lighted, the two-storied, Greek Revival mansion had massive, towering columns marching across the front and around the side porticoes. Imposing in scale, the house looked down upon Macon.

"Joseph Bond was a cotton man," supplied Zachary. "In his day, he was the largest cotton grower in the state. While the Federal troops occupied Macon, the Yankee General Wilson took this house for his."

"I don't wonder," murmured Libba.

Libba managed the introductions gracefully. Her tensions mounted as she followed Endine up a beautiful, free-hanging staircase spiraling upward past the second floor through the third floor attic to be capped by a glass-domed cupola. Twinkling stars seemed an arm's length above them.

She took off her wrap and pinched color into her cheeks, but foreboding tickled its way up her spine. She forced herself to lift her chin and march out of the sanctuary.

Daniel, handsome in white tie and tails, waited patiently at the foot of the stairs.

The ballroom, a porch stretching across the rear of the house, was a fairy-garden of rubber trees in brass containers and potted palms in cachepots of oriental porcelain. The orchestra had not begun to play, but a slender girl sat strumming a large harp. Libba's cares floated away on the quivering notes of ethereal music plucked from the strings.

"Ohh," she whispered to Daniel. "This is probably as near to heaven as I'll ever get."

Intent upon hearing every note, she sat close to the harpist whose music was lost in the babble as the room filled with party goers. While Daniel went for punch, Libba watched gentlemen and their bejeweled ladies greet one another with outstretched hands, cheek kisses, and excited cries. Shrinking into the corner, an observer, she was not part of the scene.

Her breathing ceased. Paul! Incredibly handsome in formal attire, he stood looking about. An elegant, dark-haired beauty wearing emeralds slithered up to take his arm. The fabled Victoria. Even as she winced, she felt only a twinge for Paul. Seeing them did not truly hurt.

Daniel brought a plate of food too pretty to eat. He hovered protectively. She nibbled, fearing the music. Should she merely watch the others dance?

Daniel gave her no choice. When the orchestra burst into the lilting music of Strauss, he led her to the floor. His arms tightened around her. Swaying, whirling, she was waltzing!

The world receded. There was only music and Daniel.

Cheeks glowing, Libba reveled in the strength of Daniel's embrace as they swayed to the three-quarter time. The mirrors over the mantels were angled, reflecting the dancers. Libba smiled at herself, a part of the group.

Next, a brisk cotillion set her mind spinning as she tried to keep up with the changing patterns. With elbows entwining partner to partner, she reeled. Different men smiled and flirted and squeezed, enjoying the opportunity because dancing was the only time deemed proper for a girl to be in a man's arms. Each time she rotated to Daniel, Libba tingled anew. It was only the feel of Daniel's arms, the sound of his voice whispering in her ear that made her heart sing. She wanted to dance with him forever.

Light-headed, Libba at last cried, "Enough," and Daniel took her outside. Many couples were enjoying the garden.

"I must show you the view," he said in a husky voice.

They stood at the top of the world, shouldering the stars, looking down upon the flickering lights of the city, down upon the rushing river. Suspended in beauty beyond reality, she nestled into the curve of Daniel's arm.

"Libba, my love," he whispered against her hair.

"Daniel, I . . . I. . . ." She felt afraid her heart would burst.

Leading her into an oriental summerhouse that looked like wooden lace, Daniel kissed her gently but with a great deal of affection.

Surprise fluttered through her. Paul's stolen kisses had been fraught with excitement, fear. Daniel's lips conveyed a passion springing from love. Libba responded with deep stirrings she had never known existed.

Seating her on the bench, he dropped to one knee before her. "My darling Miss Ramsey, I love you with all my heart. Will you do me the honor of becoming my wife?"

"Oh, Daniel! I love you. I do!" She began to shake with dry sobs. Her voice, a stranger's voice, was hollow in her ears. "It's you and you only that I'll ever love." Her breath came in wrenching hiccups. "But I cannot marry you."

Daniel fell back on his heels in shock. His mobile face went slack. "You can't mean that!" he said. "If you love me, that's all that matters. Of course, you can marry me!"

"No!" Near hysteria, Libba trembled violently. "Oh, I should not have led you on. You're so much fun to be with—and I do love you . . . but, oh, I'm so miserable." She buried her face in her hands.

Mystified, Daniel tried to pry away her fingers. "Tell me what's wrong. Let me help!" His hands dropped; his voice harshened. "Is it Paul?"

"No, no," she shrieked, flailing out her hands, thumping her ring against the scrollwork of the summerhouse. "It's being up here—so high above . . . all of the prominent families . . . your mother."

"Mama! She was proud of you when I brought you into

the ball. She loves you. Libba, you're not making sense."

"It's this!" Snatching off the ring, she touched the hidden spring, shook it under his nose. "This is all I know about Libba Ramsey. Your mother maintains her dignity, her station in life in spite of all her tragedy. She knows who she is. To all these people, genealogy is—everything. They can tell you every branch—every acorn—on their family trees. They have their heirlooms to remind them that no matter how hard the future might be they have a past to build on. Don't you see? I can't marry you not knowing who I am. I never allowed myself to dream you might ask me to marry you. It seemed too remote a possibility. As Endine reminded me, you are *somebody*. When you proposed, it hit me like a hammer that I have no father to walk me down the aisle."

"Is that all?" Daniel laughed in relief, but the sound strangled to a gurgle as she raised her head and he could see her face twisted with anguish.

"It's not just that—or because I have no dowry—"

"Not a bit of that matters! You're not waiting to see if Paul—"

"Oh, Daniel!" Realizing his distress, she pulled him to the bench and cupped his face in her hands. She kissed the drooping corner of his mouth and forced herself to consider him. Calming, she spoke in more normal tones.

"Forget Paul. I have. I was just a girl—in love with the idea of being in love. Yes, I was attracted to Paul—you've had crushes, maybe been in love before?" She pressed her fingers over his mouth and laughed shakily. "No. I don't want to hear about it."

"What about me? Do you love me at all?"

"At first I only thought I liked you—and I do still like

you more than any person I have ever known. Love for you has grown every time I've seen you, every time I've read your letters. You must remember that I've never had anyone to love me. I've only read books. I guess I thought love was only feelings of excitement. And pain when you weren't loved. You've showed me what love really is."

Humor drained from Daniel's face. He blew out his cheeks and spoke in cold, measured tones. "Then you're saying that I'm comfortable and safe, but Paul excited you. Libba, you've stirred my heart from the moment I saw you, but I'll quit bothering you if you don't feel the same."

"No. No, you've got it all wrong. It's just the opposite!" Libba blushed demurely. "When you kissed me just now I became a woman. You stirred feelings I didn't know existed. I'm scared. When you proposed marriage, I realized there would be children. Not knowing where I come from frightens me. What kind of traits might I pass on?"

"My darling." Daniel raised her wringing hands to his lips and kissed them tenderly. "I love you for yourself alone. That's all I need to know."

He tried to take her in his arms as if the matter were settled. She struggled against him.

"No. It's not fair to marry you. I'm not a whole person."

His arms dropped as dead weight. Sadness leadened his voice. "I thought I'd been patient. I've tried to give you time. I was waiting for this special spot. Our time. Our place."

The strains of "Auld Lang Syne" drifted from the house as the party goers rang in 1877 with the words, "Should old acquaintance be forgot and never brought to mind?"

Down below lights winked out; the restless river rushed on in its endless search for the sea.

Even the stars seemed to dim as their carriage descended from the top of the world.

In the blackness of the night, Libba lay staring upward at the protective muslin canopy of her bed at Great Hill Place. It had felt so good for this brief time to be childlike and wrapped in the arms of kindness, of love. Now a wild restlessness surged within her breast.

The words of the old Scottish melody which had ended the ball beat upon her brain. "Auld Lang Syne" meant "old long since." What old long since did she have? She rubbed the cold turquoise of her ring. Loneliness had been her way of life.

Growing up in the orphanage, each one by mutual consent had let death of family remain a wound scabbed over, never discussed. Now as she had found out what family and love could mean, her boil festered, burst. Seared with the pain, she agonized to become a part of someone in the past, to find out what she had missed.

She pressed the spring and the ring flew open. She sat bolt upright, strengthened with sudden resolve. She must take the meager clues concealed within the heart of the stone. Impossible as the quest might be, Libba now knew she would never be a whole woman until she searched for her past.

eleven

Stiff-backed, Libba fought the lurching as the train rattled over zigzagging rails. Emerging from the forest of the piedmont, the train plunged onto Georgia's flat coastal plain. These tracks held no memories for Libba. She saw nothing familiar, no friendly face at rural crossings. The tenseness which had gripped her through the wet winter and spring as the very elements had wept out her misery would not abate even though June had come at last and she had begun her trek.

She had forced herself to go back to Wesleyan to fulfill her commitment even though she had longed to begin her search.

Daniel had not been allowed for parlor visits because everyone knew he was not her brother. Their only contact had been when Dorothea Marshall arranged for her to visit Morrison Hall. Daniel had spent these occasions looking about the room at everything except Libba as she sat wringing her hands in stony silence. He tried to dissuade her from her intention to look for her father. When he saw that he could not, he offered to take her on her quest.

"No. It wouldn't be proper for us to travel together."

"It would if you married me," he responded eagerly. "I promise we'd spend the summer searching. . . ."

She had been adamant. She could not marry him without knowing who she was. Pleas exhausted, Daniel had agreed to wait, to release her until she accepted the impossibility of the task she had set for herself.

The train jerked. She tried to forget Daniel's unhappy face and instead focus on the cotton fields passing slowly like an unfolding fan. Sturdy, bright green plants, dotted with big blossoms which opened pure white and faded rose pink in the summer sun, spread before her. Jonathan Ramsey had owned such a plantation in Bulloch County, but he had not returned after the war. It lay idle, a hopeless dead end. She gave in to the tiring motion of the train fighting its way over the endless tracks. Why had she thought she could find out anything about a man and woman who were merely names inscribed in the gold of her ring?

The whistle whined a warning. Libba jumped and a startled baby at the end of the coach bellowed. A liver-spotted hound at the muddy crossroad planted his feet firmly, bristled his hair, and barked at the intruding train. Libba laughed at him approvingly. Jutting her chin, she determined to stay armed with courage. She intended to search.

A billow of black smoke floated beside the train, and an ash of charred wood blew into Libba's eye. She turned to Auntie for assistance with the cinder, glad that the competent woman was with her. She knew how to take care of everything. In a time when ordinary people remained in one county from birth until death, the Wadleys were at home on this railroad track.

Auntie produced a clean, white handkerchief and captured the cinder. "It's not much farther. I'm glad you decided not to go all the way to Savannah."

Libba grinned crookedly. "Unless we find a trail in Bulloch County, there's no use in going on. All they know at the orphanage in Savannah is that I was with refugees fleeing Sherman's bummers, I was totally exhausted, and my satin dress was hanging in rags. All I had was the ring hidden under my clothes on a chain about my neck."

Auntie nodded. "It's time to get off. For the last thirty miles the railroad has been running along the Ogeechee River. Father thought we should start our inquiries at the county seat of Bulloch County, Statesboro. We'll find something here," she said just a shade too heartily.

With a screeching of steel against steel, the locomotive turned its wheels into a long curve. *Sssst!* Steam released. The train rattled, slowed. With a jerk it jolted to a stop.

The elegantly uniformed conductor helped them down from the high step and waved goodbye. The train whistled, was swallowed up by dark pine forest.

Left in the clearing beside the lonely railroad tracks, Libba clutched her carpetbag and wailed, "I thought we were at Statesboro. There's nothing here. This is wilderness!"

"We are at Statesboro," said Sarah Lois, laughing. "Or almost. The railroad planners meant to run through Statesboro, but someone told the people that sparks from the wood burning engine would burn up the county. They made the railroad go around Bulloch. The area has remained isolated, entirely agricultural."

Undaunted, Sarah Lois hired the services of an old man with a mule and two-seated wagon. Opening their trunk, she took out long, linen dusters to protect their gray wool-serge traveling suits. Dignity intact, Auntie climbed onto the high seat, opened a black umbrella to protect them from the sun, and nodded to the white-haired man to proceed.

The wagon squeaked and bumped into a forest of towering pines. Libba's spirits plummeted, and her bonnet ribbons seemed weighted with lead.

"It's hopeless to find a trace in such an unsettled area!"

"Don't let your courage flag. We've clues to follow."

"What clues?"

"First, we know that you're the daughter of a planter rather than a yeoman farmer."

Blue eyes wide, Libba thought, There she goes again *assuming I am more than I feel myself to be*. Aloud she said, "How can you say that? This ring might not even be mine."

Sarah Lois pursed her prim lips. "Even if I grant you that, you have one thing no one could take away."

Libba raised questioning eyebrows.

"Your speech. You have a soft southern drawl, a well modulated voice, correct grammar that you learned at someone's knee when you learned to talk—before you were six when the orphanage took you in. That tells me you were born beneath a hickory not a pine."

Sparks flashed from Libba's eyes. She threw back her head angrily. Sarah Lois was being irritatingly cryptic. Suddenly she grinned, realizing her spine was stiff, her spunk renewed.

"All right. I trust your wisdom." She lifted cupped palms. "What's the answer to your riddle?"

"That's better. Bulloch county settlers on the oak and hickory lands along the Ogeechee River built plantations with many workmen. The owners were designated as planters. On the other hand, settlers in the piney woods built cabins and put cattle out to feed on the wiregrass. These yeomen led a simple, rugged life. Getting to and from market was difficult. They had little or no education. Many could not read or write. You don't have their sing-song 'geechee' dialect." She bent one eyebrow toward their driver as an example. "The matron at the orphanage said when you came you could read and write your name." Point proven, she gave a self-satisfied nod.

"All right. Where do we begin?"

The dusty road had widened into a street. The wagon lurched to a stop in front of a dwelling with gray clapboards showing through a thin coat of whitewash. A lopsided sign proclaimed: WHITE HOUSE TRAVELERS' REST. A log grocery store and whiskey shop comprised the business section. In the center of town was a square, barren except for a gnarled walnut tree beside the ramshackle courthouse.

A one-armed man who sat on a bench beneath the walnut tree was eyeing them suspiciously. Auntie cut an astonishing figure. Tall and imposing, she wore a fashionable, high-crowned Gainsborough hat lavishly trimmed with mauve taffeta ribbons and huge ostrich plumes that fluttered as she swept along. The wide brim of the black velvet hat dipped low over one snapping, dark eye and gave her a sardonic expression. With Libba, the sad-eyed waif, they made a pair to arouse curiosity.

Libba nodded at the man. He struck his whittling knife against a stick in a sharp gesture that said he had no truck with strangers. Marshaling her courage, she crossed to him.

"Good afternoon, sir."

He looked at her with watery blue eyes. Disarmed by

her smile, he spoke. "Howdy, little lady. You look 'bout as dis-gusted with our town as the Yankee who rode up to Charnock Fletcher's gate," he pointed with his knife, "and asked, 'How far is Statesboro?' "

"I thought this was States—"

"It is." He guffawed. "He was smack-ka-dab in the heart of town—three buildings and a walnut tree." He thrust his tobacco into his cheek and spat. "Patui."

Libba forced a smile. "I'm no Yankee," she replied sweetly. "I was born here. I'm Luther Elizabeth Ramsey come to look in the old courthouse records for my family. I was hoping you—I'll bet you knew my father, Jonathan Ramsey?"

"Easy enough to know everyone. Ain't but twenty-five folks here. Countin' pigs and chickens. . . ."

Once started he was hard to stop. Libba repeated firmly, "Jonathan Ramsey?"

The old man rubbed his hand over the pink skin of his bald head. "Ramsey? I recollect 'im before th' war. High and mighty he wuz. Allus chasing the almighty dollar. But the old courthouse ain't here no more. Dadburned Yankees burnt it plum to the ground."

Libba's taut smile twisted into a grimace.

"In the winter of '64, them fightin' Yankees come in here like the whole world was full of Bluecoats. The southern column of Sherman's plundering army. . . ." His voice faded to a growl in his throat. "Folks 'round here didn't leave. They stayed to pertect what was their'en. Charnock Fletcher organized hisself a army of thirty old men too old to go to the regular army. He wuz going to pertect the homes, but old Sherman had fifty thousand men. Ask Obadiah, here." He motioned to a bent old man who had hobbled up. "Obadiah clumb that there walnut tree—seed 'em coming. Got so skeered, he stayed up there three days."

"Zeke you're always telling lies on me." Obadiah protested. He removed his hat and bowed. "Don't let him upset you, ma'am. They burned the old courthouse, but Ordinary Beasley had hidden most of the records. You'll find them in the new courthouse."

"Thank you," Libba murmured, afraid to ask for another opinion of her father.

When they went inside, the ordinary gave Libba eager attention while she explained her situation.

"Are you come to pay the taxes and reclaim the land?"

"No," Libba said ruefully. "Why is the land unclaimed after all these years?"

"It's been twelve years, yes. But we're still suffering real want. Folks here abouts are far too needy to buy land, and seed, and guano. Don't know if we'll ever recover. You see, Sherman's two columns swarmed over a ten-mile swath of the county like locusts, destroying everything. Anything they couldn't pile into their wagons, they put to the torch. The Ramsey ground is still there—the dirt—I'll show you the plat. But the value. . . ." He threw out expressively empty hands.

The farm was, as Sarah Lois had said, in the oak and hickory lands along the river. Libba poured over the Census of 1850 even reveling in numbers of bales of cotton and pounds of rice Jonathan Ramsey had grown. The tax digest of 1861 showed her father among the top four landholders with 2,890 acres valued at $12,000.

Endine should see that, she thought. Her heart was beating a rapid staccato. Her father had had money, but was the old man right about his character?

Ramsey's taxes had been paid in December 1863. Here the trail ended.

They perused the dusty muster rolls for the Toombs Guards.

Names were given and sometimes places of death. They read lists of four other companies but found no mention of Ramsey. Did he not serve in the Confederacy? Had he been a traitor to his heritage? Had he been a profiteer?

Dejected, Libba left the courthouse. Auntie had gone ahead to hire a driver.

As they bumped along in the wagon, Libba read and reread the date of her parents' marriage and, glorious, glorious, her birthday. "December 14, 1858. Can you imagine knowing my birthday!"

With a singing in her blood that told her they were coming close to discovery, Libba leaned forward, not noticing the lurching of the wagon. They were moving toward higher ground beneath a canopy of overarching live oaks.

"This be the Ramsey place," said their guide.

Stretching before them was a long, damp, mossy lane. Magnolia trees, planted close together, formed an allée of black-green leaves. Creamy blossoms, wide as dinner plates, exuded heavy sweetness that filled Libba with sadness.

Sobered into silence, unbroken save for the squeaking of the wagon and the clop-clop-clop of hooves, they stopped expectantly at a break in the ground-sweeping magnolias where a shrub garden marked a path.

Climbing down slowly, Libba stooped to pick up a leaf

and hold it against her cheek. She started down the holly-
and-boxwood-defined trail that led through the woods,
willing Auntie and the guide to let her walk it alone. A
brick wall warned her of what was to come.

The family cemetery housed many well-marked
graves, but her attention focused immediately upon the
granite obelisk at the center.

With her fists clenched against her mouth, she read:

Luther Elizabeth King
Well-beloved wife of
Jonathan Ramsey
born Savannah February 12, 1840
died Bulloch County
December 14, 1858

Grief overwhelmed Libba. She had found her mother
only to lose her so quickly. Goose flesh prickled her cold
arms. She felt rather than saw Sarah Lois standing outside the wall.

"My . . . mother . . . died the day I was born. Oh,
Auntie, do you think she ever saw me? Did she hold me
in her arms—even once?"

"Oh, she must have." Tears streamed down her plain
face.

Steeling herself, Libba glanced over the markers
which commemorated her forebears, here a Salzburger
seeking religious freedom, there a Revolutionary War
hero. She would come back and commune with them.
For now she must deal with the grief of seeing her
mother's grave. Whatever had happened to Jonathan, he
did not lie beside his wife.

Summoning all her strength, Libba retraced her steps to the road and pressed on down the dark avenue. Stark against the sky, brick chimneys towered two stories high, standing at either end of a blackened pile of rubble that had been Magnolia Springs. Within the lumpy mass of sooty ashes, a piece of metal arched grotesquely. Stepping over the crumbled foundation, Libba surveyed her home, struggling to remember what her mind still blocked out. Stirring a sour smell as she kicked through the ashes, she picked up a pottery bird. It meant nothing. Auntie found a cast-iron skillet.

Near the fireplace—a fragment. Libba pounced upon it. The flesh on her thighs turned cold, seemingly sloughed from her bones. The porcelain head, crackled, burned blue-black, stared at her with black eyes and pursed red lips.

"Sudie!"

Groping for support, Libba's hand slid down the chimney, slashing on the rough bricks. Face in the ashes, she sank into the blackness.

twelve

Black smoke plumed against the winter sky above the towering chimneys on each end of Magnolia Springs. Panting, Libba ran toward the house as fast as her stubby, five-year-old legs would carry her. The terrifying sound of drums beat louder, louder. She dropped Sudie, tripped, fell flat.

With her breath knocked out, she lay dazed. Up ahead her playmate turned. His chubby black face became all eyes, white, rounded with horror. He ran back, tugged at her limp arm.

"G'up, Libba," Joshua lisped. "Wun!"

Scampering for the safety of the log kitchen behind the tall white house, the children did not understand what sort of demons were behind them. They only knew that for three weeks distant drumming had sent the grown folks scurrying about hiding things, hauling bales of cotton to the swamp, burying barrels of syrup in holes in the ground as they whispered fearfully of some strange monsters called "Sherman's bummers."

Outrunning Libba into the steamy kitchen, Joshua flung himself against his mother, rooting beneath the canopy of her white apron. Libba followed him, and the long limbed woman cuddled her equally close.

"Hush yo' crying, chirrun. Old France won't let nothing harm you."

Bustling into the kitchen, a tiny wisp of a woman with thinning white hair drawn back severely from her fine-boned, transparently pink face, bent to kiss Libba. Patting the child absently, she spoke in a breathless voice.

"Do you have the rotten eggs ready, France?"

"Yes, Miss Nannie."

Libba followed her grandmother into the chicken yard. Looking about furtively to make sure her movements were concealed, Nannie went inside the rickety fowl house and dug a hole in one corner. Surreptitiously, she slipped an ebony and ivory box from the folds of her black taffeta skirt. Libba stood on tiptoe to watch as she opened it. She loved to look at the twinkling jewels.

Nannie took out a turquoise ring. "You've seen this ring before. Your father had it specially made for you. Watch me now. I want you to remember its secret." She pressed a carved gold flower. The ring popped open. Pointing to the plaited hair preserved beneath glass, she said, "This is a lock of your mother's hair. She was my daughter. And, see. Your mother and father's names."

With her lips clamped firmly together and her eyes forced wide to hold back tears, Nannie threaded a gold chain through the ring and fastened it about Libba's neck.

"Keep this hidden beneath your dress. It, and the teaching I've given you, might be your only legacy."

Nannie put the jewel case in the hole. Packing the earth, she covered the spot with straw, made a hen nest, and added the rotten eggs. She grabbed the feet of her maddest setting hen and plopped her on top to guard. Brushing off her hands with a self-satisfied smile, Nannie put a finger to her lips.

"Shhh, Libba. Don't tell a soul. Now. We must get you cleaned up. We shall look like southern ladies when our guests arrive and trust that our dignity. . . ."

They went upstairs where Nannie scrubbed her freckled nose. Libba stubbornly insisted upon brushing her hair herself. Suddenly, she heard Nannie's intake of breath and ran to stand beside her looking down into the yard.

Horsemen in blue coats rode through the gate, brandishing swords and firing pistols into the air. They demanded of old Augustus, the man-of-all-work, the whereabouts of the Rebs. Screaming and yelling, they rode round and round, tearing down the chicken yard palings and the split rail fence that kept the cows out of the corn.

Trembling, Libba clung to Nannie through the deathly stillness after they had gone. Suddenly the yard filled with another group, quieter, wearing blue coats with gold braid.

With her back ramrod straight, her head proudly erect, Nannie greeted the men with dignity. They stamped up on the porch with their saber scabbards dragging, scarring.

"Good evening, officers, may I give you directions?"

"You can save yourself trouble, old woman, if you hand over your valuables and make us a good meal."

A red-headed man came around the corner of the house. Grinning and holding out a silver tray and tea service, he said, "Lookee here! This little feller showed me what grows in rose gardens these days."

"It seems you have found my valuables," Nannie said regally. "If you care to wash up—and clean your boots . . . I will fix your supper."

"Here." The red-haired man shoved the tray at Nannie. "You serve it yourself and on *our* tray." He laughed and spit on the porch, splattering them with slimy, brown tobacco juice.

Libba stamped her foot and whispered loudly, "Joshua, you shouldn't tell! These are Yankees!"

Bewilderment sagged his cheeks. He had obeyed. He dragged his toe in the dirt.

Noticing Libba for the first time, the ruddy soldier grabbed her. Instantly, her pet goose hissed, darted across the yard with his long neck extended. Swooshing toward the offending hand, he pecked.

Screaming, the man fell back in surprise. Honking, the goose attacked him. The soldier kicked out with his heavy boot.

"No. Nooo!" Libba screamed, throwing herself on the enemy. "Gandy's my friend!"

Flinging Libba away, he kicked, kicked, kicked. Expelling air in a plaintive honk, the goose fell dead.

France appeared, scooped shrieking Libba under one arm and dumbfounded Joshua under the other. The terrified woman ran with the struggling children to the sanctuary of the kitchen.

Libba hid behind the velvet draperies in the dining room angrily watching the rude men make Nannie wait upon them herself instead of sitting at the head of her own table. Hugging the soft rag body of her doll, she rubbed Sudie's cold porcelain head against her hot cheek and immersed herself in the fury of hating every man dressed in blue cloth. With Gandy gone, Sudie was her only friend because there sat Joshua on the Yankee's knee.

Nannie had returned outside to the kitchen and France

had come in with a tureen of stewed chicken—or was it Gandy? The soldiers suddenly focused their attention upon the tall woman. With her head wound in a bright red turban, France wore her best dress, a stylish hoop-skirted black satin.

"You there!" The soldier stopped France. "Your mistress put you in her dress to save it, didn't she?"

"No, sir. This my Sunday-go-to-meeting."

"You lie!" Whipping his knife from his belt, he lashed out, slashing the satin skirt.

The porcelain tureen crashed to the floor spilling its contents—whatever they were —across the oriental rug. Screaming protests, France danced in frenzy with the satin fluttering, shredding from the flashing knife.

Nannie flew into the room. The tiny woman pulled back her servant who towered over her. Furious but without hysteria, Nannie said, "I demand that in my house, you behave yourself like gentlemen."

Mumbling about showing uppity little Rebs a thing or two, the soldiers prepared to leave.

Old Uncle Augustus was commanded to drive a mule in their wagon train. Taking a fancy to Joshua, saying he could fetch and carry for them, the red-haired man swung the stunned little boy up on the wagon and drove away.

France's screams terrified Libba. She clapped her hands over her ears, but she could not shut out the chanting wails.

In the blackness of the night, a candle flickering, a furtive whispering awakened Libba. Tiptoeing across the hall, she peeped in. Nannie and France were folding back the feather bed. They laid a shivering Joshua on top of the hard-packed cotton mattress. Commanding him to lie still, they flung the pliant feather bed over him. Carefully, they spread the sheets and counterpane so that the bed looked smooth.

Libba padded into the room, dragging Sudie.

Nannie jumped at the sound. "Shhh, Libba. Joshua ran away when the soldiers weren't watching. My guess is, they'll come looking for him. You stay in bed and pretend you are asleep. Nothing looks as innocent as a sleeping child, and . . . France go back to your quarters. Just cry so much you can't tell them a word."

Lying immobile, Libba clung to Sudie. She clenched her teeth as the sound of heavy boots, of crashing furniture, and breaking china rang through the big house. From the yard, chickens squawked, pigs squealed, shots echoed.

In the morning dead chickens sprawled everywhere. Strewn hog carcasses lay spoiling with only the hams cut out.

But the exhausted little boy still slept, made up into the feather bed.

Nightmares and daylight hours merged. More Bluecoats came, demanded food, took valuables until there was nothing, nothing.

Libba sat in the parlor close beside the smoldering fire talking to Sudie. A rock hit the floor beside her with splinters of crackling glass. The lace curtain flamed. Terrified, the child dropped her doll and ran screaming. Voices drew her to the veranda where Nannie stood demanding, cajoling, pleading with men who threatened her with flaming torches.

Torches flung through windows turned furniture into flambeaux. Nannie snatched Libba roughly, ran, dragging her away from the roaring inferno that had been home.

Tears streamed down Libba's face as she struggled to free herself from Nannie's grip. "Sudie. I left Sudie."

"Hush, darling. Oh, where are France and Joshua? She's too handsome a woman for her own good. We must run. Don't cry. We'll go to Miss Nicy's. Surely the Yankees will spare so fine a house as Bird's Nest."

They stumbled along the short-cut path to their nearest neighbor. In the darkness, they collided with a fleeing servant. Cyrus reported that the courthouse in Statesboro had been burned. Men with torches were circling Bird's Nest.

"We must—run for the river," Nannie gasped in short breaths that gulped air. "With no bridges across the Ogeechee—maybe the river will stop the wagon trains. If they cross, it will be at Rocky Ford. It's so dark! Cyrus, can you find the place where the mail is rowed across from Screven County?"

"Yes'm."

Libba felt herself being lifted in the hard-muscled arms of the tall man she could hardly see in the darkness. With her head bumping his shoulder, she fell asleep. She awakened as he laid her in a rowboat. She looked up at exposed tree roots dangling grotesquely from the high bank over her head and whimpered. Nannie's arms tightened comfortingly around her. Libba could feel the thudding of Nannie's heart.

Cyrus carefully dipped the oars, and the boat slipped silently beneath boughs of dark green live oaks. Gray beards of Spanish moss, hanging nearly to the water, brushed their faces with hairy tendrils.

A beam of moonlight riding the middle of the river had to be crossed. All three held their breaths until the boat was once again hidden by the lush vegetation on the opposite shore.

"Thank you, Cyrus," Nannie said. Pressing her hand against her chest, she panted, "I can't go—any farther—but even Sherman's army can't be—everywhere. We should be safe in Screven County. In the morning—we'll find the railroad."

Cyrus cleared a sheltered spot in the thick forest and before he left them built a small fire against the cold of the December night.

Libba wept for Sudie. Lacking the doll's comfort, she found her thumb. Sucking noisily, she went to sleep.

Awakening, Libba looked into Nannie's face, pinched and blue but smiling in determination as she combed her white hair with her fingers.

"We must make ourselves presentable before we get on the train," she said in a determinedly cheerful voice. "The Central line is not far. I'm sure Wheeler's Cavalry is protecting it. All of the southern newspapers say that Sherman's men are ruined and lost, fleeing for their lives to the safety of their fleet on the seacoast."

Gauging their position as the red ball of the sun broke through the eastern mists, Nannie headed due north toward the rail line. Struggling for breath, she had to stop for rest. The sturdy child watched her with frowning, slant-eyed glances.

A cloud of black smoke billowing above the treetops

made Nannie clap her hands in glee. "We're saved,
Libba. See. What did I tell you? The train has stopped to
wood up."

Eagerly, they hurried forward. Voices drifted on the
still morning air. Strange, clipped voices, some speaking
in foreign tongues, startled Nannie, and she clasped her
hand over Libba's mouth lest she give their presence
away. Trying not to cry, the snuffling child could not
understand what had suddenly struck her courageous
grandmother with terror.

On hands and knees, they peeped from beneath a bush.
The smell of turpentine burned Libba's nose. Black
smoke, sinking in the oppressive air, swirled low.
Bluecoat infantry clustered along one side of the railroad
track that was to have taken them to Savannah, to safety.
Libba heard a shout of command.

As one man, they lifted the line of rail and ties as high
as their shoulders. At another command, they let it drop
heavily, shaking loose many of the spikes and the chairs
from the rail joints. The men seized the loosened rails
and used them as levers to pry off the rest. Piling cross
ties like kindling wood, they set fire blazing.

Tears streamed down Nannie's cheeks, and she retched
violently.

With frightened fascination, Libba watched the men
lay the iron rails crisscrossed over the fire. They stood
back, wiping sweat until the rails gleamed red hot in the
middle. Gleefully they lifted the ends and twisted rails
into great iron knots. Other men, shouting to better this,
carried the rails to wayside pines. Laughing raucously,
they wrapped the hot rails around the slender trees, skin-
ning, searing, causing turpentine to drip.

Nannie lay weak, sick. Libba shut her eyes. Still she could see the pine trees with rails looped around them like pretzels. The backs of her eyes burned with the fearsome image.

Too terrified to cry, Libba wiped Nannie's face. Her teeth chattered. Libba pressed her warm little body over her in an effort to stop Nannie's shivering. Warming, they remained in each other's arms until a shout roused them.

"General Sherman is coming."

"Hey, there's Uncle Billy, himself!"

They peered out. The soldiers snapped to attention as Major General William Sherman, a man with hard, cold eyes and a cropped beard, dismounted from his horse. His orderly handed him a flask of whiskey. He took a long pull.

"Well done, men. I congratulate you. We have devoured the land. The people retire before us. Desolation is behind. To realize what war is, one should follow our tracks. War is hell."

Nannie and Libba crawled away.

"That snake-eyed Sherman!" Nannie spat out the words with hatred. "I'm afraid his funeral pyres of our railroads are also the death biers of our noble cause."

The child could not understand her grandmother's words or her reaction of defeat, but watching her, Libba seemed to see Nannie's spark go out. Kissing her blue-veined hand, Libba sensed that she was the stronger and determined to help her.

When they stopped to rest, Nannie promised safety in Savannah. "We have friends and relatives there, Libba. We'll get a message to your father. You'll like Savannah. It's beautiful—fine houses—parks—spreading live oaks. We'll be happy again. Keep that little chin up. You'll see." Lulled, they slept in a warm spot of sunshine.

Libba awakened screaming. Smelling turpentine until she tasted it, seeing railroad tracks twisted around pine trees like pretzels, she thrashed wildly.

With trembling hands, Nannie comforted her from her dream.

The nightmare returned each time she slept. Images blurred, tumbled, merged over long miles. Nightmare and daydream became indistinguishable. Running in the wrong direction, seeing the whole horizon lit with campfires, seeing wagon trains with men throwing on stacks of fodder or kicking in cribs of corn without even stopping, seeing the conquering army crossing their river on pontoon trains, they despaired.

They joined a group of refugees, women and children, moving toward the haven of Savannah. Libba had to feed Nannie because she could not reach her mouth with her shaking hand. Near the mouth of the Ogeechee River, they hid in a rice mill huddled together, silent except for babies crying.

"Libba." Nannie drew her close with cold, cold hands. "I'm confused. I've lost track, but it must be near your birthday. You will be six years old. A big girl. You must be a big girl. You must not cry anymore!"

"Yes, Nannie." She nodded her curly black hair. Solemnly she rubbed the blue hands. Pulling rice straw around her, she repeated, "I'm six now. I won't ever cry again."

The night was suddenly bright with rockets.

When morning came, the refugees could see Fort

McAllister plainly across the salt marsh. The Confederate flag was fluttering in the breeze above the earthenwork fortification. The weary women cheered.

Their voices choked midword. Shot rained from Parrott guns across the river toward the fort. Heavy shot fired back across the marsh. Then all became quiet as a Sabbath.

A blue-coated signal officer, waving his flag from a platform on the ridgepole of the rice mill on the left bank, made them remain hidden. They heard a commotion in the fort, musket skirmishing in the woods, then quiet.

The sun was fading, and Libba piled more straw over Nannie.

Signal flags wigwagged. Troops rushed out of the fringe of woods that encompassed the fort. The lines, dressed as on parade with colors flying, moved forward.

Fort McAllister came alive with big guns belching forth dense smoke enveloping the assaulting lines. One color went down, but it was up in a moment.

Libba's nose burned from the sulfurous smoke. There was a pause, a cessation of fire. Smoke cleared away. The parapets were blue with swarming men firing muskets in the air, shouting so that the watchers heard, or felt they did, that Fort McAllister had fallen.

Libba crept back to Nannie. How could she have gone to sleep in all that noise? Libba wrapped her small arms around Nannie and tried in vain to warm her cold, still body.

"I love you, Nannie," she whispered innocently against the waxen cheek. "I promise I won't ever cry again. But I wish I had Sudie."

thirteen

The chimney wavered drunkenly in Libba's bleary gaze. Lying in the sour ashes beside the brick pillar, she shivered even though the summer sun beat down upon her. Cold water touched her lips. A strange woman was bathing her face with water from a shard of pottery. *Who?* Libba brushed aside cobwebs of memory. Something was in her hand, a cold, hard object. Straining to lift her jelly-muscled arm, she held it up, squinting.

"Sudie," she whimpered.

"You frightened me," said Sarah Lois. "You've been in a faint a long time."

Strength did not return. Libba responded numbly as they helped her to the wagon. Dozing, fainting, she ran from dreams. Voices penetrated her darkness. Hands lifting. Funny dream. The hard wagon had become a soft feather bed; the cold spring water, steaming herb tea.

Strengthened, she fluttered thick lashes, gazed myopically at a canopied bed.

"What . . .? Where?"

"Shhh. Just rest," Auntie whispered. "I sought aid at a neighbor's house. She was your mother's friend. Sleep. She'll tell you all you need to know in the morning."

June sunlight streamed across Libba's bed, but she remained in a cold fog of taunting, teasing dreams. At last she forced herself to move. Immediately a maid appeared with steaming coffee and buttered toast.

131

When she felt sufficiently fortified and presentable, Libba descended the stairs. Auntie and a plump woman sat chatting as cozily as two old friends.

"Good morning," Libba said.

Their hostess turned and her soft cheeks lifted in a smile of delight. "Good morning, my dear. Refreshed?"

"Libba, this is Mrs. Nicy Bird. We are guests in her home, Bird's Nest."

"How do you do? Thank you so much for your kindness."

"Not at all. You have brought excitement to the summer doldrums. Do sit down. My, my, you don't look a bit like your mother, Betty. Except you are dainty. You don't have Jonathan's big nose, thank goodness, but you have his hair. Black, unruly curls always fell over his forehead. See, there! He had that same habit of raking them back."

Libba stayed the involuntary motion. This voluble lady would bring her family to life. She pushed a footstool close to Mrs. Bird's feet and sat cupped, waiting.

Mrs. Bird described the young couple, so much in love, the dark curls and the fine, blond hair bending to cut the wedding cake.

"Leaving for their honeymoon, they followed the tradition of crossing the river at Rocky Ford. It was legendary for the girl to feign fear of her horse stumbling so that the one she loved could take her in his arms, and step by step, from rock to rock, carry her to the opposite bank. Many couples have known the thrill of crossing upon the rocks of the Ogeechee."

Libba clapped her hands in delight. Throughout the recital of stories, she interrupted only once to ask, "Did my mother live to see me?"

"Yes, dear. She would not let us take you from her all that day. She kept kissing your fuzzy head. She nursed you even though her strength was waning. The doctor could not stop her hemorrhaging. That night she slipped from us. Jonathan was wild with grief, inconsolable. France Handshaw became your wet nurse. You grew up with her Joshua as a playmate. Betty's mother, Amanda King, came to raise you."

Nannie. Libba cherished the memories that had come pouring over her amid the ashes of Magnolia Springs. She held back the rushing flood because the woman's voice was babbling on.

"Jonathan became another person. He had been a Christian lad as a youth, but he fairly worshipped his beautiful wife and took too much pride in his home. When she died, material possessions became his god. He threw himself into raising tremendous crops of Sea Island Cotton which grows only along this coast and is highly priced in world markets."

"Money came so easily. It didn't satisfy. Oh, he was still charming, laughing, using funny old sayings, but his heart was hollow. He turned to humanism, thinking he had no need of God. He indulged himself, traveling restlessly."

"What you're avoiding saying. . . ," Libba swallowed a bitter taste rising in her throat, "is that he had no love at all left for me. Did he blame me for my mother's death?"

"I don't think he blamed you as much as he blamed God."

Libba had drunk too much of pain. Her heart seemed to fill and swell and ache within her chest until it could hold no more. At least Nannie had loved her. Nannie's great heart must have strained like this until it simply could pump no more. Nannie had left her saying, "You're a big girl now. Never cry." Libba gritted her teeth and tossed back her hair, but the room reeled. She felt weak, sick with all the remembering.

Mrs. Bird sensed her sorrow. "Enough talk. Let's walk in the garden. The daisies will lift your spirits."

As they strolled around the old house, Sarah Lois asked, "How were you lucky enough to escape?"

"Sherman's bummers demanded I leave the house, but I refused to get out of bed, telling them I had just borne twins who had died and been buried. Someone torched the house with me in it while others dug in the fresh dirt thinking I was lying and had hidden valuables. When they uncovered the bodies of my babies, they were remorseful enough to come back and extinguish the fire. But, oh, they left the little graves uncovered!"

Libba's hatred boiled, spilled over, caught flame. How could her father have been so callous that he left her with only her frail grandmother in such a dangerous place? Enmity for Sherman became enmity for Jonathan Ramsey.

"If only he had run this way! Nannie might not have died if we hadn't been running in the wrong direction."

"There was no way to know. There was a sea of Bluecoats between us."

Libba could not rest. Over their protests she returned to Magnolia Springs.

Walking over land that should have been her legacy, Libba longed for her home. Rampant with weeds, diminished by encroaching forest, the fields, nevertheless, held promise in their rich loam. She was surprised at the intensity of feeling the smell of this earth, the greenness of these trees evoked.

Paul, defending her against Endine, had marked her as a southerner. Looking pridefully at Magnolia Springs, Libba knew she had a trait of which she had not been aware. She possessed that fundamental southernness: love for the land.

Little good it will do me. Brooding, she poked and searched among the ashes of her past.

Over the supper table, they tried to speak of pleasantries, but the question that had chewed at the edges of Libba's heart could remain unanswered no longer.

"Was my father a traitor?" she blurted. "We did not find him listed in the local army companies."

"No. You've gotten the wrong impression. He was away when the war began. He wrote Nannie that he realized too late that he had neglected you. He had a part in organizing the Confederate Navy. He was a blockade runner—and he wrote once about some new thing—iron ships which would change all the navies of the world."

"Didn't you ever see him again?"

"No. Well—I believe it was the summer of '61. He sent for a ruby necklace and ring that had belonged to his mother. He hoped Nannie would understand that he'd fallen in love with a woman who reminded him of Betty. He wanted an engagement gift—said he'd come home before he married."

"And . . . and he never did?"

"We never heard from him again. No, wait. That spring after Lee surrendered, a private detective came 'round.

Said Jonathan had been wounded in an explosion. They had to amputate a foot. Said he'd been sent to search for you. Of course, you and Nannie were gone without a trace."

The clacking of the train along the track filled Libba's ears and muted the voices from her past until she found the strength to consider them. A faint smile lifted her cheek as she visualized the much-loved young girl who had been her mother. She kissed the turquoise ring. Its hidden lock of hair had now become her pearl. Staring unseeingly out of the window as Georgia's sandy, low country became again red clay hills, Libba cherished her new-found remembrance of Nannie. Mercifully, her mind still blotted out the moment of her realization of Nannie's death and the strangers who had taken her from her dead grandmother's arms. Her eyes filled and her chin trembled.

Sarah Lois patted her hand. "I could teach that Nicy Bird a thing or two about tact."

"She painted my father as having no love for me. But how could he have left me in the path of—"

"No, now. He thought you safe and well-cared for. No one dreamed the war would take that course, and—"

"But she made him sound a reprobate. She finally did remember he survived the war—but with an amputation. With what she said, I feel I am also less than a whole person."

"You're forgetting one important fact. He sent someone searching for you."

"Yes." It was a small sound. Libba turned her face to the window. Night was falling. Flickering lights along the way filtered through mist. Suddenly it was dark, and the glass mirrored her drained face. The coach hurled through blackness as if it were a separate entity from the present world.

Behind her the hum of voices rose to a chatter. Passengers who had traveled all day stiffly ignoring the strangers around them reacted to the darkness, reaching out to one another, needing friendly talk. Shrinking from her need, Libba withdrew into her own cold depths. At last she let the clacking rhythm of the rails carry her from pain toward sleep.

Great Hill Place welcomed them home. The boisterous family enveloped them. Realizing Libba needed time with her grief, they let her spend several days in quietude.

Finally the sunshine beckoned her. Seeking seclusion, she descended the granite-lined path. She plucked a fragile flower and buried her face in the spicy-sweet perfume. *It smells like orange blossoms,* she mused. The thought opened Pandora's box. Around her swarmed Daniel's promises that she had kept locked in a back corner of her mind.

She had reached the paved circle in the center of the garden. Sinking to a bench beside the sculpture of the winged Greek messenger, she yearned the more for Daniel as she listened to a bird calling across the still air. The lonely sound received a joyous answer from some dark corner of the forest.

"Oh, Hermes," she said to the statue paused in flight. "Can't you wing a message to Daniel?"

"Perhaps he did, for here am I."

Startled, Libba wondered if in her fanciful mood she was dream-wishing Daniel's voice. Half-afraid, she turned.

Daniel stood there. Unaware of his own manliness and charm, he warmed her with a smile that lit his face with love. Running into his outstretched arms, Libba burrowed against him in childlike need for comfort.

They sat on the bench, and Libba told him of her search. Unburdening her heart of the hurtful details which she had been able to share with no one else, she ended with a wail, "Oh, if we hadn't been always running in the wrong direction, I might have Nannie now to love and care for."

"But aren't you glad you remembered something of her love?" Daniel kissed her clenched fingers. He tried to draw her closer. "I don't mean to press you, my beloved, but aren't you ready now to marry me—to let me care for you?"

"No, Daniel!" She pulled her hands away. "My heart is too hollow. My family came to life only to die. I feel as if I had been to a funeral."

Daniel saw that she needed to weep and release her grief. As he had done that first day they met, he pulled his face into a mask of tragedy and spoke in comic register. "You'll feel better if you cry."

"No," she snapped, jumping to her feet. "No! I told you of my vow to Nannie."

"You know she didn't mean. . . ." As Libba turned her back and isolated herself, Daniel pounded his fist against his thigh. Frustrated, he flung out, "Don't be foolish, Libba."

"Don't call me foolish!" Wringing her hands, she cried

out in misery. "I hate Sherman, and oh, Daniel, I know it is heretical, but I hate my father!"

"But don't hate me!" The tragedy of Daniel's drooping eyes and mouth were no longer a mask. "Don't shut me out." He held out his arms. "Let me love you!"

She could hear a sharp edge in his voice warning her that even Daniel Marshall's infinite patience was wearing thin, but she eluded his reaching arms.

"I can't forgive my father for not loving me. What—oh, Daniel, what if we had a child, and I couldn't love it? You can't marry me. I'm only half a person!"

"Nonsense. Oh, Libba, think! Think about the love you and Nannie shared. You've had a tragic experience, but many people have suffered. God did not promise that we would not suffer, but that He could turn the suffering to—don't run away from me," he pleaded, hurting as badly as she.

"Libba," he called after her as she plunged up the stone steps. "Don't keep running in the wrong direction!"

fourteen

Running from Daniel, fleeing from herself, Libba was overtaken by a rigor that rattled her teeth. In her emotionally weakened condition, she could not fight a severe case of grippe. To her nightmares was added a fevered dream of stumbling through a maze, always bumping against a dead end. She burrowed beneath the quilts and railed at Daniel's God. Her hate-hardened heart blocked out His reply.

Auntie dosed her with Farmers Fever Pills and herb tea. At last Libba was able to sit by the window and look outward for the first time in weeks. Against the verdancy of a June day, a cardinal cocked a merry eye from the bough of a creamy rose. Senses quickening, Libba tried to capture the image, but poetry would not come. She thought only of blood and snow.

When Auntie came in, Libba shared her decision to remain an old maid devoted to teaching.

"You're fulfilled with the life of a spinster."

Auntie pursed her prim mouth. "Yes, but I enjoy my position as chatelaine of Great Hill Place. I feel valuable to my father—" Embarrassed, she shook the streamers of her cap.

"I imagine when one's father is a great man, it's impossible to find a suitor who can measure up," said Libba.

Auntie's dark eyes snapped. "Libba! You're placing too much import on who and what your father might be! God made each person unique. He gave us the freedom of choice in what we shall become. You are special. Don't shut yourself away. Daniel loves you—Paul, too, I suspect."

Libba's blue eyes clouded. Daniel had not returned. She was not vain enough to think Paul had postponed his engagement because of her, even though the discovery of her background made her an eligible catch.

When Libba was well enough, she was summoned to Colonel Wadley's study.

"I have been making inquiries from your neighbor's facts."

What facts? Libba wondered.

"I may remark that I have made a check of the East Coast, but no one knew a blockade runner named Ramsey. Since Mrs. Bird mentioned iron ships, I went to Hampton Roads, Virginia."

Libba blinked uncomprehendingly.

"It was there that the important naval battle was fought between ironclads, the *Merrimack* and the *Monitor*.

"Yes, sir."

"Ramsey's name wasn't recorded as having served in the Confederate Navy along the East Coast. This means that your search should now be—"

"Forgotten?" It came out a squeak. "Oh, I can't sir. I must keep trying."

He smiled approvingly. "Forgotten? No, indeed, but I may remark that you seem to have acquired gumption and grit."

Grinning, Libba tossed back her sooty curls. "Yes, sir! What do you suggest?"

"That you write inquiries about Confederate naval officers."

"Thank you, sir."

Each day Libba posted more requests. Each mail brought disappointment. Weak with despair, she threw up her chin and began again.

When Wadley returned and discovered Libba had received no information, he said, "What you need, young lady, is a trip. We shall take a family excursion to Columbus."

Libba thought, *At least I can put off facing Daniel.* Columbus's factories had supplied the Confederacy. Perhaps she might find information about her father. Quickened hopes as quickly died. Second only to Sherman's holocaust of Atlanta had been Wilson's burning of Columbus.

Colonel Wadley had sent Paul to work in the office in Columbus. What if Daniel thought she was leaving him and going to Paul?

The exuberant Wadley family filled the train to the nearby town. They remained in a state of secret excitement until the next morning when they went to the wharf on the Chattahoochee River.

A sparkling white steamboat waited on the building ways. Emblazoned on the hubs of the paddlewheel was the name *Rebecca*. All was in readiness for the launching of this addition to the Central line, the largest and most beautiful ever built to ply the Chattahoochee.

Happy at Miss Rebecca's pleased smile, Libba wondered why the surprise included her. She had seen dry-docked, ocean-going ships with deep-draft, curved bottoms. This riverboat was flat. Realization crept over her. Boats were different. Water was different, but they all meant sailors. What if her father had been in the navy here?

Hopes fell as she looked around. Everything was too new. She could see the building of the *Eagle and Phoenix Mill* with its white phoenix rising symbolically.

After much ado, Captain Whitesides shouted through a megaphone, "Ready for launching. Cut the ropes!" He broke a bottle of wine over her bow as the *Rebecca* slid swiftly down the building ways.

Paul appeared and pinched Libba's arm. "Now we've completed business. It's time for your surprise, little one."

"What do you mean?" Libba drew away.

"Iron ships," Paul said cryptically. Laughing at her blank face. The navy yard in Columbus constructed— among other things—the *Muscogee*, an ironclad ram."

"Ships of iron!" exclaimed Libba, suddenly luminescent.

"Catesby Jones, hero on the *Merrimack*, came here to command the CSS *Chattahoochee*, and. . . . Anyway, I'll take you to the newspaper office to see what we can find in the files."

They turned through page after page of yellow, musty newspapers until they came to a *Columbus Daily Enquirer* article which told of the ill-fated attempt at launching the ironclad *Muscogee*. It made no mention of Ramsey. An aside in the story described the *Chattahoochee* as being at the wharf for repairs.

"Perhaps your father merely saw the *Muscogee* but served on the *Chattahoochee*?" said a reporter who was helping. "Here's another story: 'The ram was launched

December 22, 1864, but when the Union cavalry laid waste to Columbus on April 16, 1865, the Yankees set her afire. She burned to her waterline.' The gunboat, *Chattahoochee*, escaped. Her crew set fire to her to keep her out of the enemies' hands."

"Then that's a dead end, too," said Libba sadly.

"Not necessarily, ma'am," the reporter said. "The *Chattahoochee* led two lives. Earlier in the war the gunboat exploded and sank. She was raised and repaired. Let's look further back in the files."

The horrifying story leaped from the pages of the June 7, 1863, *Columbus Daily Sun.*

"Pandemonium followed on the *Chattahoochee*. Fourteen men were killed in the blast or died immediately afterward. Those who had been scalded ran about the deck frantic with pain, leaving the impression of their bleeding feet and sometimes the entire flesh, the nails and all, behind them."

With her fist against her mouth pressing back nausea, Libba read the names of those killed. Jonathan Ramsey's name was not listed.

" 'The graves of these men are in the town of Chattahoochee, Florida. Wounded were transported to the hospital in Columbus,' " she read aloud.

Libba wiped her sweating face. She felt weak and ill from her constantly fluctuating emotions.

"Names of the wounded aren't given, but I have another idea," said Paul. "Let's go to the city clerk's office."

"But if the town burned, wouldn't the records be gone?"

"Some enterprising soul usually remains calm enough to save the records." In the post registrar of sick and wounded soldiers, they found the names of the patients in eight hospitals.

"Oh!" Libba wailed. "The web is just too tangled."

Paul whooped, "Listen to this! 'On May 21, 1861, the Ladies Soldiers' Friend Society organized. They operated the Soldiers' Wayside Home at the corner of Broad and Thomas Streets. When the gunboat *Chattahoochee* exploded, the victims were brought here to be cared for.' There's a list!"

"Jonathan Ramsey!" they chorused.

No information was furnished on recoveries, but the clerk told them the dead had been buried in Linwood Cemetery.

There in the southwest corner of the graveyard they found markers for the victims of the explosion. With dying hopes, Libba knelt to read the tombstones.

fifteen

Daniel Marshall had never felt so unsure of himself. Walking through the sun-dappled woodland that led to Great Hill Place, he tried to let the quietness seep into his soul. He enjoyed being alone with nature and with God, but his attempts at prayer about Libba had become strivings.

Listening to the callings of the birds, his heart yearned for Libba. He would never have wealth like the Wadleys to bestow upon her, but he could take care of her. He was ready to make a home, to begin life with Libba.

Waiting on the stoop of Great Hill Place, he saw her a last! His eyes sought hers beyond the span of assorted Wadleys noisily returning home.

Libba looked so tiny, alone in their midst. Daniel's jaw twitched over clenched teeth. Paul was handing her down from the carriage.

She lifted her chin in that endearing gesture of courage and caught the tenderness, the pain on Daniel's face before he could mask it. Moving shyly toward him, she held out her hesitant fingers, coming short of touching him. She spoke huskily. "Hello, Daniel."

Auntie, perceptive as always, shooed the children pawing Daniel for a story and said firmly, "Libba, why don't you take your guest into the garden while we all get settled?"

Walking stiffly apart, they started down the stone steps. The memory of how she had run away from him blocked words; they could think of nothing to say.

Daniel, struggling not to rush her, held himself in check until they reached the center of the garden before he spoke. "Did you find a record of your father's service?"

"Yes." It was a small, dead sound. She was surprised he had known the Wadleys' mission. "He was wounded when the *Chattahoochee* exploded. We saw some graves. There wasn't a tombstone with his name. We plan to look in a graveyard at Chattahoochee, Florida, where the accident happened."

Her words, her coldness, were shutting Daniel out. "We," she had said. She and Paul? Would it be best if he went away and left her alone? Leaning over her, feeling more anguish than all of the trying experiences his life had brought him, Daniel struggled to understand her pain.

"But Libba . . . why graveyards? Mrs. Bird said a detective looked for you after the war. That would mean—"

Libba blinked. "Yes. I suppose he survived the war. I've felt so miserable, I forgot about her saying that. I did bring back some names to write, but—oh, Daniel, I don't know that I care to keep trying." Her hand waved toward his chest.

Relief, joy spread over Daniel's face. "You know it doesn't matter to me!" He opened welcoming arms for her.

Shrugging away from his grasp, she stepped backward. "I do remember Mrs. Bird said he didn't love me. I can't forgive that."

Daniel threw back his head in exasperation and rolled his eyes heavenward. He dropped to one knee before her. Tilting her pointed little chin with one finger so that she must meet his eyes, he spoke softly, patiently as to a child.

"Libba, you are judging your father. The Bible says we

must not judge. You don't know his side. If he's a reprobate, that doesn't matter. It doesn't change who you are. What matters is you are letting unforgiveness poison your soul."

She tried to twist away, but he held firm.

"No! Listen to me. Jesus said, 'Judge not, and ye shall not be judged: condemn not, and ye shall not be condemned: forgive, and *ye* shall be forgiven.'"

"Don't preach me a sermon! You're judging me!"

Daniel rocked back on his heels and waited. Praying for her, bathing her in the warmth of his love, hoping God's words would sink into her soul, he rejoiced when her face softened. Slowly she raised her arms toward him.

"You're right, Daniel. You are right! There is no room in my heart for love. I have to forgive!"

With a passion she had never before released, Libba flung herself into Daniel's waiting embrace. He buried his face in her dark cloud of hair, then held her back to search her eyes.

"Yes, Daniel. I love you. I do."

Laughing, he caressed her face. Libba returned his kisses. Keeping his arm around her lest she flee, he fumbled in his pocket.

"How did you know we'd be back today?" she asked.

"I didn't. I've been coming on the noon train every day. It made me feel closer to you. I've been afraid that Paul would beat my time—"

"I told you there was no need to be jealous of Paul."

"Then it's time I marked my claim, woman!" Daniel said in a bass voice that was meant to be funny and strong, but shook. He took out a large, square-cut diamond. "I'd be honored if you'd wear my grandmother's ring."

"Ohhh! It's beautiful. I love it! I love you. But I'm still— I'm just afraid—I'm not ready—"

Daniel placed a finger on her lips. "I wish we were married this instant—but I love you too much to press you. Just wear my ring. Say we're betrothed. Let me help with your search."

Unable to speak, Libba extended her hand. Tenderly Daniel slipped the ring onto her finger and kissed her hand. His laughing eyes met hers, joined. He gathered her into his arms for a kiss that sealed his commitment.

Letters coming in answer to Libba's inquiries to former members of the Ladies Soldiers' Friend Society of Columbus plucked her tightly strung nerves.

At last she opened one from a Mrs. David Hudson that read in part:

> *Many of the worst patients were transferred to the gangrene hospital in Eufaula, Alabama. Perhaps Dr. Hamilton Weedon of that city would remember, although he treated a sad multitude of cases.*

Mrs. Bird had mentioned amputation, but it seemed useless to write to a harried doctor. This was probably another dead end.

The letter she had saved until last bore the signature, Mrs. Daniel Morrison Marshall. She recalled her panic when first she received a note from Daniel's mother. She was not ready to be badgered about an engagement party with this obsession for finding her father, and she ripped open the envelope with her temper at the ready. The brief note said: "I must see you at once. Come as soon as possible."

When Libba arrived at Morrison Hall, she found Mrs. Marshall's quiet manner replaced by jumpiness. Without preamble, she led Libba to stand before an oil painting depicting a sailboat on the building ways. Libba cocked her head to one side as she stared uncomprehendingly.

"It's luminous. The silvery gray shines like opal, but. . . ."

Mrs. Marshall tapped the signature. "It's here. The key. It was here all along. Cowles Myles Collier. Your father's friend. Oh, what a mystery it is how our lives entwine if only we take the time to notice how we touch others!"

Libba was blank.

"Myles Collier. A navy man. There when the *Chattahoochee* was being built. Oh, I apologize for not thinking sooner. One thinks of oceans not rivers when one thinks of navies. I didn't know the extent of Collier's service, but—" She burst out laughing. "I'm babbling. Wait! Here comes my neighbor from High Street. She can explain it all!"

Libba turned to meet a woman with masses of auburn hair.

"May I present Mrs. Richard Hines, the former Miss Georgie Shackelford."

"I'm delighted to be of help," Georgie bubbled. "I knew Jonathan well."

Libba brushed back her tumbling black curls in amazement.

Georgie clapped her hands. "That was his habit, too. You are his daughter! You look like him instead of your mother."

"You knew my mother?"

"No. I knew Emma Edwards who was in love with him. Emma, a willowy blonde, confided in me that Jonathan said she was exactly like his dead wife, all pink and blue and gold."

Libba winced at the thought of her father in love with another woman, but she drank in the details of the story this gracious lady related.

"Our plantation, The Pines, was a haven during the dreadful times of war. The gunboat *Chattahoochee* was being built at the Saffold navy yard in Early County, Georgia, and the officers visited us frequently. My twin, Hannah, married Myles. I married Richard."

"And Jonathan? Did he marry Emma?"

"He kept saying they'd marry as soon as the South won the war. He seemed to recover from the wound he received in the explosion. Evidently the infection was deep in the bone. The last I heard, the sickness had returned, and gangrene had set in."

Pieces were beginning to fit. Libba did not know if she could face the picture they made. Twisting her hands, she thought of dear Colonel Wadley. *Grit and gumption, Libba*, she said to herself. *Gumption and grit.*

Georgie fumbled in her reticule. "I wrote to Hannah and Myles because he and Jonathan were close friends. Ah, here it is!" She extracted a letter.

Libba skimmed Collier's kind words about her father. At least someone thought well of him. He wrote about Jonathan's dare-devil adventures as a blockade runner at the Gulf port:

> *When the war ended, Jonathan was being cared for by Emma Edwards in her home, Barbour Hall, which had been converted into a hospital. He refused to have his foot amputated. I regret that I*

> haven't kept touch with Jonathan. Ellen and George
> moved to California, but they would have written me
> if Jonathan had died. I'm certain you'll find him in
> Eufaula.

Georgie smiled sweetly. "Captain Harrison Wingate and
his vivacious wife, Lily, Emma's niece, were also our
guests at The Pines. The Wingates are prominent in
Eufaula society. Perhaps you read the newspaper accounts
last fall about the race of the steamboat named for their
daughter, Mignonne?"

Libba felt numb, "I recall the excitement. Everyone
was talking about it. I had no way of knowing that my
father—"

"And everyday," Mrs. Marshall broke in, "I saw Myles
Collier's sailboat and did not connect him with the navy."

Daniel arrived. He bounced around the room unable to
contain his excitement. "You'll write to Eufaula?"

"No. I cannot bear another letter. I must go. See him for
myself. The Wadleys are going to Columbus for the trial
run of the *Rebecca*. Colonel Wadley mentioned business in
Eufaula. Everything is pointing there."

"I am going with you!"

September gales had raised the river. The Chattahoochee tumbled over the falls at Columbus in its rush to
the sea. Daniel realized that the water lapping beneath the
gangway to the *Rebecca* was making Libba dizzy on the
springing plank. He reached to steady her, but Paul, on the
deck, pulled her aboard.

The *Rebecca* resembled a floating palace. Three stair-
step decks turreted by a glassed pilothouse were adorned

with wooden-lace trimming on every available overhang. The dazzling boat commanded the attention of everyone on the wharf.

"Will we get to Eufaula today?"

"No, little one," Paul said. "We came on board to test the new electric lights. We will lie at the wharf tonight. Eufaula is eighty-five miles south. It will only take thirteen or fourteen hours to get there."

While the others toured the boat, Libba sank down on a velvet settee in the grand saloon, pleading a headache.

"Alone at last," said Daniel. "I had thought a romantic river cruise would make you fall so madly in love with me that you'd succumb and be ready to marry." He gave her the look of a sad-eyed puppy. "I'm beginning to have my doubts."

"Oh, Daniel! You promised not to press. I really have a headache, and being on this elegant boat makes me feel so insignificant. I'm terrified. I don't want to see my father. And . . . what if he's dying? You know that the alternatives of gangrene are amputation or death.

"Darling, you'll feel better if—"

"Don't you dare say if I cry!"

"No. No. If you'll find your father and forgive him. You'll never be satisfied if you turn back now."

"But how can I endure it until we get underway?"

Daniel slid a comforting arm around her shoulders, but Libba remained as hard and unyielding as the stiff-backed sofa.

Dinner was a multi-coursed meal served with flourish. Colonel and Mrs. Wadley dined with the ship's master, while the younger group was hosted by the mate.

When the warm September night was dark, the party went on deck to witness the test of the new electric lights.

Daniel stood back in the shadows watching. The gray streaks in his dark hair stood awry in little plumes like the pinfeathers of a ruffled bird. Libba's eyes, like those of everyone else, were fastened on Paul.

Conscious of the crowd's attention, Paul dramatically turned on the switch that pulled apart the hard-carbon sticks in the arc lamp. An arc of brilliant white flame formed between them.

"Ahhh!" came an intake of breath from the crowd as the night became bright. In contrast to the brilliant white glow, light from the kerosene lamps in the cabin and the gaslights on the street corner faded into nothingness.

"That was the Brush light," Paul announced. "Next is the light of the United States Electric Company, a bull's-eye, the same as used on locomotives."

After a long discussion, it was decided that the steamer would use both. Even though the inventor had not declared it perfected, the Brush light would be tried in the place of the flambeaux which had been used when landing or loading. This would prevent danger of sparks setting the cotton afire.

With the test over, Libba bid Daniel a hurried goodnight and disappeared into the stateroom.

Daniel had anticipated a stroll in the moonlight after those infernal electric lights were out. He told himself her indifference was merely trying to block out the pain of tomorrow's discovery. Pacing the darkened decks alone, he wondered if she had been judging the two men. Surely she could see that his love and Paul's were not the same.

sixteen

Darkness smothered Libba, blacker than ever after the brilliancy of the electric lights. She fell into exhausted sleep only to awaken to empty silence. Having abandoned her childish nighttime prayers, she felt utterly alone.

She had nearly found Jonathan Ramsey. Why should he want to meet her? She'd be of no interest to him. Worse. A bother. Probably she deserved the treatment she had received. Torturing herself throughout the night, Libba looked out as dawn broke over the Georgia shore. They were still at the wharf. She had hoped the journey had passed in the night and she would have less to endure.

After breakfast, Daniel led Libba to the deck and produced a banjo. He sang a funny ballad about a maiden on her maiden voyage on the fabled steamboat, *Rebecca*. As the group gathered around them, leaning in to harmonize, Daniel twanged his voice, twisted his eyebrows, and launched into the disaster song, "Lost On The Steamer Stonewall."

Laughing, everyone leaned in close to harmonize on the popular song which immortalized the steamboat disaster.

By nightfall, the *Rebecca* was still far from her destination. The merry group dressed in elaborate evening attire. After a sumptuous meal, they danced in the mahogany-floored ballroom. Paul claimed a waltz with

Libba, but she was relieved when Daniel took her on deck and she no longer had to keep a false smile.

"Oh, Daniel, how much farther?"

"Have patience, my dearest. Tomorrow."

"What if my knees are too weak to walk the gang-plank?"

"I'll be with you every step of the way. You can always know that for the rest of your life."

Libba gazed at Daniel's dear face in wonderment. She moved into his arms and lifted her lips to kiss him with gratitude.

In the stillness of Sunday afternoon, the steamboat glided into the wharf at Eufaula, Alabama. Libba and Daniel hired a carriage with Sarah Lois as their chaper-one.

Libba had not wanted to consult the Wingates or look for Barbour Hall and the blond woman unless forced. Dr. Weedon would be easiest to find.

As they rode down Randolph Avenue, Libba felt in-timidated by the grandeur of the mansions. "I've never seen such houses. They go up, up, up."

"Can't you picture ladies on those widows' walks watching the river for wayward husbands? Ah, that sounds like a song." Daniel plinked an imaginary banjo.

Climbing the steps to the Weedon house, Libba's knees shook. Daniel and Auntie both supported her.

A man with a graying mustache assessed them with snapping eyes. "Bring her right into my office."

"Oh, no, sir." Libba's voice was a husky rasp. "I'm not a patient—" She realized there was swelling around her eyes. Her hands and ankles were puffy. She spoke more strongly. "I'm sorry to disturb your Sabbath rest, but I'm seeking information about a naval officer wounded on the *Chattahoochee*. I'm told he was sent to the gangrene hospital here—"

"You must realize the blockade had us cut off from supplies, and we were treating dying men with herbs and bark and using carpenter's tools for surgical instruments."

He called his wife. "Mary, these people are tracing a naval officer who was my patient. I'm trying to warn them—Whom did you say you—"

"Oh, I'm sorry," Libba said quickly. "This is Miss Wadley and Mr. Marshall, and I am Elizabeth Ramsey. My father was Jonathan Ram—"

"Can it be?" Mary Weedon exclaimed. "Those black curls. It must. . . ."

Wordlessly, Libba snapped open her ring and held it out.

Mary Weedon clapped her hands. "Of course, we know him. I must run tell them immediately."

Paling, Libba shouted, "No! Please!"

"Wait, Mary!" Dr. Weedon said. "Jonathan's detective found no trace. They assumed you dead. This will be a shock. We must prepare him."

"Yes, please. I'm not ready to see him. I doubted he was alive. I'd heard he was dying—refusing amputation. . . ."

"Yes, he was dying. Hatred and pride were poisoning his soul even as the infection in his foot was poisoning his blood. He was willing himself to die."

Mary broke in. "With Emma's love and prayers, he let God into his life. With her as his wife, he's a changed man."

"When he allowed me to amputate, his health became good."

"Last summer he felt God calling him to preach." Mary consulted the watch pinned to her bodice. "He'll be preaching soon. Do let me tell him before he leaves for the church."

"No! Promise me you won't tell him. He may not want to see me." Libba began to wring her hands.

"Of course, he does," said Mary, wiping tears.

Daniel spoke in his professor's voice. "The man wouldn't be able to preach after such a shock. If you'll kindly direct us to the church, we'll slip in. Libba can get accustomed to seeing him before she introduces herself."

Before he let her go, Dr. Weedon pressed his stethoscope, a short wooden rod, against Libba's chest. He pulled at her eyes and examined her cold fingers.

"Young lady, you are suffering from a case of simple stress. You are bottling your emotions within you. The most beneficial thing I could prescribe would be a good cry."

They waited in the churchyard until the services had begun. They slipped into the back pew, and Libba cowered behind the man in front of her. Only when Jonathan Ramsey began his sermon did she move to see the man whose presence she was trying to shut out.

Dark laughing eyes swept over her as he included the strangers in a humorous remark. He raked back a tumble of black curls, sending waves of emotion vibrating through her.

Daniel stretched his arm along the back of the seat in a message of his surrounding love. She smiled wanly and forced herself to look back at the man in the pulpit.

The preacher was not handsome. He had a bulbous, red

nose. His face was heavily lined but pleasantly set as though he took joy in his religion. The silly man was talking about how to boil a frog. For a moment she let herself listen to his jovial voice.

"If you throw a frog into hot water, he will jump out. To boil a frog you place him in cold water. Make him comfortable. Then warm the water just a tad. He won't notice. Add more heat—more heat. He accepts it. Suddenly the water is boiling. It's too late!"

The congregation laughed.

"It's the same way with sin. We. . . ."

Libba followed his glance to a placid woman with silver streaks in her pale blonde hair. *Precious Emma? How could he marry someone else who looks like my mother?*

The woman tapped a wiggling lad of about ten. Her child. His! The black curls were unmistakable.

My half-brother. She tried to summon feelings of love, joy. Guilt overwhelmed her. All she could feel was jealousy. Jonathan cared for his son, lived with his son. He did not love his daughter. He had blamed his daughter for her mother's death. He had left her. Beads of sweat crawled on her upper lip.

Music. The closing hymn. People standing.

Libba fled.

Daniel found her retching beneath a giant oak tree.

"Do you want me to talk to him first?"

"No! I can't speak to him. I can't forgive him. Take me back to the boat."

seventeen

Libba lay in her bunk shaking.

Auntie spoke tartly. "For two days I have let you wallow in misery. You should be the happiest girl in the world. Drink this tea. Then go out and speak with Daniel. He is stricken that you've refused to see him."

"I should send him away forever," Libba stormed. "Don't you see? He's gentle—has so much love to give. He deserves someone better. My heart is too cold."

"Nonsense! This tea will warm you."

Swallowing the bitter stuff, Libba longed to see Daniel, yearned for the comfort of his arms. If only they were married. Part of her wanted to be his wife, to bear his children, but something was missing. She had no joy. Demoralized by the aching void that her father did not love her, she felt unable to function. She'd leave Eufaula. She had seen him. Wasn't that enough? She'd return Daniel's ring—she loved him too much to hurt him. *I'll devote my life to teaching. I'll prove myself worthwhile to some student.*

Sarah Lois filled the cabin with the strength of her presence. Helping Libba to dress, she pushed her on deck.

Daniel saw Libba's swollen eyes and little blotched face and bounded to her side. His gray eyes were big, round hollows. His voice was liquid with emotion. "Let's go up on the hurricane deck."

The top deck afforded privacy. Hurting for her, Daniel

tried to shelter her in his embrace. Her stiffness made him drop his hands. She did not need him as he needed her.

"Libba, I know this is hard, but you make me want to shake you. I understand that growing up unloved is tough. But you must know that early neglect, whether real or imagined, is not insurmountable. It can build character—as it has in your case. We all admire you so much."

He turned away, hurting so badly he did not want her to see. His voice dropped until it was nearly blown away on the breeze. "You were doing well until I asked you to marry me. Do you find that so distasteful? Do you want me to release you from our engagement? To go away and leave you alone?"

"Yes, I've been thinking that would be best."

Without looking back, he walked away.

Libba ran down the deck and hurled herself against his hunched back.

"No. Daniel. No! I couldn't bear life without you. I love you. I do."

He looked at her with a grave, vacant face, waiting.

"I needed to know who I am. I've found Jonathan Ramsey. It doesn't help. My insides feel torn, bleeding. He's a hypocrite! Preaching about love when he ran off and left his daughter. A silly sermon. Boiling a frog, indeed!"

"I liked it—and him. There's truth in his humor." He kissed her gently on the forehead. He wanted to be more than her mentor, but he saw that he must restrain his passion and try to give her love. "Perhaps he's not the knight you hoped to find. But you're lucky. Most orphans of this war will never know who or what their fathers were. Even we with fathers find that earthly fathers often fail."

"He gave up searching for me!"

"But God never gives up on us. He sent His Son, reaching out, searching for each one of us to be part of His family. You haven't found peace . . . because it is your Heavenly Father you must find and accept."

Libba wriggled free of his grasp. "I was baptized as a child," she snapped, "but God doesn't care any more than Mr. Ramsey does." She jutted a defiant chin. He did not reply, and at last she relented. "All right. How do I find your God?"

"The first step is confronting your father, forgiving him."

She gripped the rail. From this pedestal, she looked across the treetops, down to the rushing water. "I'm confused. Where are we? Which way are we going? Back to Columbus?"

"Not yet. We headed downriver making adjustments on the machinery. Now we're heading back to Eufaula. We should reach there Wednesday afternoon. *Oh, Libba,* he thought, *I'm confused, too. Which way are you and I going?*

"Probably he'll have prayer service. Will you take me back?"

"You know you must speak to him this time?"

"I know." Libba faced into the wind.

The turquoise ring shone on Libba's finger as she walked into the church and took a seat half-way down. All of her ill feelings tumbled about, bumping, pulling, exhausting her.

The service was over at last. People were standing. Libba sat. Swallowing, she feared she would be sick. Daniel's hands, strong, sustaining, lifted her, guided her toward the door.

The preacher was shaking hands. He wavered before her as a bright blue blur.

Why did he have to wear blue cloth like those Yankee fiends he left me and Nannie to face alone?

Suddenly she could see the image of the enemy soldier kicking, kicking, kicking until Gandy lay dead.

Daniel would not let her flee. The moment had come.

Libba stood face to face with Jonathan Ramsey.

Coldness froze her heart. There was no forgiveness in her.

She could not speak. She could not lift her hand.

She sagged against Daniel. Surely he would speak, bridge this silent gap. She waited. No one could do this for her but she, herself, yet she was too weak.

She prayed, *God, if You're out there. If You really do care, help me! At least I can take his hand and speak, but I don't have any feeling. Help!*

Her hand moved. It met the big, calloused grip of the man who had stood waiting. A wonderful warmth gave healing power to her body. She lifted her face, smiled.

Jonathan's hand pressed her ring. His red face crumpled as he gazed at her in wonderment. He turned her hand over, touched the carved gold flower that released the mourning ring's secret. The turquoise opened. Jonathan kissed the glass-covered lock of plaited golden hair. Tears streamed over the ridges of his face. He smothered Libba in a hug.

Dry-eyed, stiff-backed, she said, "My name is Luther

Elizabeth Ramsey."

Everyone was crowding around, patting, hugging, talking without being heard.

Numb, Libba nodded acknowledgment to introductions. The blond woman, Emma. Plain! What did she think! That placid expression concealed her emotions. She spoke in a quiet voice as she introduced her son, Wingate Ramsey. Handsome Captain Harrison Wingate; his twinkly-eyed wife, Lily; Harrison, Junior, and the black-haired, porcelain-skinned Mignonne were presented as family. Libba was being transported to a place called Barbour Hall.

The carriages rolled up the drive to an Italianate mansion crowned by a glassed belvedere. Painted brown velvet and ermine, Barbour Hall sat like a comfortable dowager with a welcoming look.

The double doors were thrown open. Like a picture framed by the glowing side lights, a beautiful woman with a dazzling cascade of red-gold hair stood waiting. Her beauty was enhanced by an inner glow of contentment. Near to bearing a child, she rested her hand on her protruding stomach with obvious joy.

Adrianna Edwards greeted Libba warmly. "I'm delighted to have you all." Her words lifted with a rising inflection that carried the sound of her smile.

The extended family swirled about Libba ready to pour out love, but she stood isolated, lonely.

Daniel was asking Foy and Harrison Wingate about the big race won by their steamboat, *Mignonne Wingate*, as the group gathered around the dining table.

After they had eaten supper, someone voiced the question in all of their minds, "Where have you been all these years?"

Libba began her soliloquy in a whisper which caused them to lean forward as she related the events of the enemy's capture of Magnolia Springs and her subsequent flight. She enunciated every heart-rending detail, feeling grim satisfaction when Jonathan wiped tears and pushed away his bowl of peach cobbler. She sat back, relieved of the lump in her throat, and ate the sharp, juicy pie with relish.

"It's a miracle you survived," Ramsey said. "I had given you up for dead. I wasn't physically able to go myself—and somehow I could not bear to see Magnolia Springs. I hired a detective who found no trace. I had given up all hope."

Libba thought, *You had given me up long before that.*

"And now you have made our family circle complete!" The lilting voice belonged to Lily Edwards Wingate, Foy's sister, Emma's niece. "Since Foy and Adrianna have so beautifully restored our parents' home—and now the promise of an heir to carry on the name—only this part of Emma and Jonathan was lacking." Lily's face glowed with contentment from being cherished by the handsome man who sat with his hand upon her shoulder.

Libba's troubled eyes met hers, and Lily, perceptive to the needs of others, added quickly, "We've claimed you for our own. We haven't given you a moment alone. Why don't you and Jonathan walk in the garden?"

Relief and fear dueled. Libba nodded mute thanks to Lily. Trailing her fingers over Daniel's sleeve in reluctant parting, she followed her father to the back porch.

Jonathan negotiated the steep steps stiff-legged, struggling with his cane. Libba stood back, waiting. He led her to the summerhouse. "Let's sit," he said gruffly. "My knees don't want to carry me."

For the first time Libba forced herself to look at the stump of her father's leg. He walked on a wooden peg fastened below the calf with leather straps. Fighting to suppress a shudder, she said, "I was afraid you might not want me to interfere with your new life."

"How could you think that?"

"You didn't once check the orphanage."

"At the war's end, I was out of my mind with illness from this foot. It was Emma who thought of hiring a detective—she longed to have you as our daughter. Most orphanages had not been built. Churches began building them to care for the orphans left by the war."

"Bethesda Orphanage was there since 1740."

"But I heard that orphanage suffered loss to Sherman and was in ruins until Colonel Wadley took charge—"

"You know Colonel Wadley?"

"Everyone knows of his reputation. No one dreamed an old woman and a child could travel that far. I reckoned without the backbone of Amanda King. I'm proud to see that you've inherited her determination. This could not have been an easy quest."

"No."

"You're disappointed in what you've found. You're not ready to claim me as your father. What proof—"

Libba pushed back her unruly curls with their shared habit. She laughed ruefully. "It's not proof. I couldn't forgive your not searching for me. I see now I was wrong. Daniel has asked me to marry him. First, I had to know about you—who I am."

"You have no memory of me nor I of you. I couldn't

forgive myself for that either. I loved your mother possessively. Had tremendous pride in her beauty and my home. I worshipped money. Things it would do for her. I won't lie about my character to make you proud. When I was a child, I accepted the fact that Jesus died for my sins, but when I reached my teens, I fell into what I thought were good times. I let material possessions became my god. When my Betty died, I lost everything."

"You had *me*. Did you blame me for her dying?"

"No. You were a bundle in a blanket that my grieved mind didn't think about. I blamed God. Sometimes with grief there is a terrible anger. A frustrating, futile anger. I didn't have a wife anymore. So I had nothing. I turned to humanism, indulging myself.

"I was yearning for spiritual things that I couldn't possess. My soul was panting, but it could not rest. I was seeking but never finding, journeying yet never arriving." Tears trickled over his rough cheeks.

"And you never thought of me at all?"

A strained silence stretched between them.

"When I came to Eufaula, my life began to change. Mignonne, a beautiful baby, was the center of everyone's love. I began to long for you, to plan to marry Emma and take her back to Magnolia Springs as a mother for you."

Eyeing him doubtfully, Libba said nothing.

"Then came the war, and the world turned upside down. Our cause was lost, my home burned, my child dead. I planned suicide."

"Suicide?"

"I almost threw myself into the Chattahoochee."

"What changed your mind?"

"Emma's love. Emma's prayers. When I let Jesus into

the ship of my life, I was immediately at the land whither I went. My searching was over. A new life had begun."

"So you became a preacher?"

"Not then. God had work to do on me. Last summer I saw Adrianna struggling for direction and realized that many people need to turn back to the Bible as a guide for living. I felt the call to preach."

Daniel's caring face was framed in the arch of the gazebo.

"I'm sorry to interrupt, but everyone wants to go back with us to see the *Rebecca*."

The Wingates and Edwards offered so much love that Libba felt more guilty at her resentment of Jonathan Ramsey's son, Win.

Colonel Wadley welcomed everyone aboard and invited Libba's new family to get acquainted with her by being his guests for a cruise.

Everyone agreed as enthusiastically as if they had never ridden a steamboat.

eighteen

Uhmmm! Uhm! Uhmmm! The *Rebecca's* whistle echoed and reechoed as she prepared to leave Eufaula. Steam chu-chooing, black smoke billowing, the steamboat quivered with the thrill of departure. On the bottom deck, standees ranged around and on nine hundred bales of cotton. Lifted high above them on the stateroom deck, one hundred twenty passengers filled to capacity this maiden voyage in regular trade. Businessmen strutting with black coattails flapping, women clutching spreading hats abloom with flowers, and children costumed with richly adorned clothing like miniature adults waved at those unfortunates left ashore.

The Wadleys had returned home, but with Libba and Daniel at the rail were Lily Wingate, Mignonne, and Beau; Jonathan, his wife, and boy. Instead of joy, Libba felt she must endure the cruise. Then she would return to teaching.

The sternwheel swished, turned, lifted a spray of water. Faster, faster it caught the rhythm, propelled them forward. Libba's emotions churned like the water wheel.

Piercing music from the calliope on the hurricane deck peaked the enthusiasm of the throng. From across the water another steam organ played a shrill staccato. The sleek *Mignonne Wingate* shot smoothly forward tootling a competitive battle of the calliopes. The group on the *Mignonne* began to sing. The *Rebecca's* passengers, hanging over her rails, screamed the champion roar.

Scrunching her shoulders against the noise, Libba witnessed a private scene. Lily threw a kiss to her husband in the *Mignonne*'s pilothouse. As he saluted her, love linked them, making them one, at peace above the chaos. Their tangible warmth made Libba long for the fire of such love. Why had she kept denying Daniel? Her hand groped for his but found nothing.

Daniel was gone. Passengers disbursed. Libba was alone.

She could no longer put off facing Jonathan Ramsey's blond wife and his black-haired son. She joined them on the front deck.

Eagerly, Emma made a place for her.

"How nice of the Wadleys to give us this trip to get acquainted," Emma said, soothing the situation. "It's special for us to go back where we courted. We'll show you."

Libba did not want to hear, but Emma's including smile made her relent.

They reminisced about the Shackelford twins being wooed by Myles and Richard, and Libba explained how Daniel's mother had made the connection between Collier's painting, her neighbor, Georgie, and the Ramseys.

"When people take the trouble of loving and caring about one another, things connect in a marvelous way," agreed Emma.

"Why, you've almost quoted an Indian proverb Daniel shared with me 'All things are connected.' "

Jonathan nodded sagely. "The rains fall, the rivers rush to the sea, evaporate, begin again. All the waters of the world connect. When they don't—when they're blocked—disaster reigns. Life changed when we could not go beyond this river. We were getting barefooted as a bunch of yard dogs when our cotton plantations were shut off from England's factories by the Yankees. Let me tell you about my daring blockade runner days."

When Libba returned to the stateroom she shared with Mignonne, she wrote down what her father had said.

"Waters of the world connect."

A line in search of a poem, she thought. She sifted her brain for words, images. None came. *I'm beginning to feel better toward him—them. Can he forgive and accept me?*

Libba chose her blue ball gown. Mignonne helped her tame her curls into a fashionable coiffure.

"Daniel and Paul will be overwhelmed with your beauty, and your father will be proud!"

For the first time in her life, Libba felt pretty. Maybe at last she could please those who had rejected her.

Libba entered the grand saloon eager to see—and be seen by—Daniel. Descending the steps of the ornate staircase, Libba glanced about. She had not seen Daniel since they came aboard. Was he avoiding her? With the guilt she carried for all the wrongs she felt she had caused, had she driven him away? Was he jealous because Paul Morley was arrogantly asserting his authority as representative of the steamboat line?

"The penalty for being punctual is that one must always wait for others who are late." Lily joined her unbidden.

"I guess I'm constantly waiting to be punished."

Lily's smile did not fade. "You were raised in a strict, legalistic atmosphere with a strong sense of right and wrong. Sometimes people like that watch themselves, thinking they must work to achieve perfection and forgiveness, but God is not like that. He reached down for us in love when He sent His son to achieve our forgiveness. All we need do is accept the gift. Let Jesus into your heart, and He will take away your burdens and fill your life with joy."

Lily's insight brought tears flooding to the surface. Wanting to pour out her heart, Libba could not. Dr. Weedon was right—and Daniel. She needed to cry. But she had held her tears too long, she could not let them go.

Uninvited, Lily could say no more.

Diners were drifting in, and Daniel appeared at last. With his hair neatly cut and combed and his black formal evening clothes immaculate, he was more handsome than Libba had ever seen him. He smiled at her as if she were the most beautiful, desirable delicacy of all.

Course after course was served. From a teacart laden with sweets, Libba chose a napoleon and swapped Daniel a bite for a taste of his eclair.

To walk off the meal before the dancing began, Libba and Daniel strolled the deck, oblivious to other passengers. From the hurricane deck, the sobbing of a gypsy violin sent shivers of music trembling over the water.

A discordant note set Libba's teeth on edge. Emitting from within the heart of the great boat, a mournful sawing and scraping twanged a quivering foreboding.

"We've stopped," she gasped.

"Yes, my lovely one." Daniel laughed. "Even a floating palace must stop for wood to fire those monstrous furnaces. And to pick up freight to pay the bills." He pointed to the stevedores lifting more bales to add to the lower deck.

"More? The boat is loaded already. Look how tattered those bales are. The cotton's wasting." She leaned over the rail. "See? Locks are floating down the stream like little ducks."

"Some old farmer has been saving those shabby bales, waiting for a rainy day. It's amazing how that new electric lamp floods the river with light. They say people who see the boat approaching think she's afire."

Libba stiffened with alarm.

Daniel cuffed her chin. "It's safe. The machines for generating the lamp's fluid are worked by steam from the boilers. The electric light does away with the danger from flaming torches. There'll be no more fires in this age of electricity."

The orchestra began playing the summer's most popular song, "Whisper You'll Be Mine, Love." Daniel hoped the moment for romance had come. "May I have the honor of this waltz?"

They stepped into the ballroom. Dancers made a kaleidoscope of colors as they swirled.

Paul came striding toward her. Grasping her bare shoulder, he gave her a knowing wink and whirled her away over the waxen floor before Daniel could protest.

Libba awakened sweating. Bolt upright, blinking in the blackness, she smelled smoke. Probably her old nightmare. But there had been no railroad tracks knotted like pretzels. Of course, there was smoke above a steamboat. Trying to relax, she relived the passion of Daniel's kiss stolen in the shadow of a lifeboat before he walked her to her stateroom. He had urged her to postpone their marriage no longer, to give him a definite answer. Why had she not?

Mignonne groaned. Something was bothering her, too.

Libba stood up. Smoke! Black! Thick, hot! Real smoke!

She opened the door. "Fire!" The dreaded word, the curse of steamboats. Bells clanged. Whistles shrieked.

Grabbing their wraps, Libba pulled at the sleep-drugged Mignonne. "We must save our parents. Our brothers. You get Lily and the boys. I must help my father. He can't run." She choked on smoke that smelled like burning rags. Eyes smarting, she stumbled toward her father's stateroom. Swirling smoke confused her. Lost, she sank to her knees to get a clearer breath.

Scrubbing at her streaming eyes, she suddenly released a flow of cleansing, long-pent tears. *Oh, God, I am lost.*

And suddenly she knew. They had all loved her so much, had tried so hard to help her, to bring her face to face with God. The moment had come. Only she, herself, could do the rest. Only she could remove the cold hard stone she had placed over her heart and open the secret place.

Crying for mercy and forgiveness, she prayed. *Oh, God, I know now I can never be good enough to come to One so holy, but You have come in to me. Strengthen me now. Help me to save my Papa. Oh, my Heavenly Father, save Daniel.*

A quietness came over her. Her mind cleared to think. *Count the doors. Third from the corner.* She banged on the door. Jonathan answered. Flinging herself into his cabin, she fell upon him sobbing.

"Oh, Papa, I was lost. I couldn't find you in the smoke. I thought I'd never find you!"

Her father's tears mingled with hers as he kissed her tenderly. "My little daughter. How I've needed you!"

Weeping, they held each other. Nothing else mattered.

Emma's arms encircled them, urging them up. From her deep reserve of inner strength, she murmured words of direction.

Flames were spreading. Nothing could be saved. There was no time to find and strap on the wooden leg.

Sharing the burden of the crippled man, the two women timed their strides so that he could swing between them. Steady, calm amid people rushing madly by, they gained the deck. Gale winds blew fresh air to anxious faces, relieved stricken lungs. The winds fanned the flames, sending them leaping across the cotton bales on the deck below, consuming everything. Captain Whitesides, running with an ax preparing to scuttle his boat, suddenly dropped it in despair. The fire had gained too great a headway.

"The cargo can't be saved," he shouted to his crew. "Save the passengers!"

People were rushing from the cabins, jumping into the river, piling upon those who had been standees on the freight deck. The mass of humanity struggled to swim and keep themselves alive.

The dry cotton, burning like powder, sent flames leaping up to the cabin deck, threatening the huddled family.

"Looks like Judgment Day," Jonathan said with a laugh as one of the officers handed him a cork life preserver.

Libba stared at her father, then laughed. Freed by forgiveness, warmed by love for him, she knew that now she could leave everything to God's Judgment. Circumstances and the natural failings of humanity had driven her father. She would no longer judge him. She would love him and remember that her own character was as it was because of what he had been.

Screams glanced off her as she moved with the surging crowd. Feeling the turquoise ring, she knew her father had loved her without knowing it. Even in his grief, he had given her this clue that had enabled her to search.

Libba helped her father and Emma into a lifeboat and

turned back into the blaze crying out for Daniel. She had put him on a pedestal, fearing she could never be good enough for him. Now she understood he loved her just as she was, in spite of her shortcomings. She stumbled toward his cabin.

Oh, Daniel, I wish I had not put off marrying you. Dear God, don't let it be too late!

Daniel found Libba's stateroom engulfed in flames. Wild with grief, he covered his face to plunge in, but something tugged at his brain, telling him her door was open. She must be out! Crawling to Jonathan's door, he found it open. Fiery timbers were dropping around him.

Daniel stood up, ready to run. A falling rafter grazed his cheek. Stunned, he fell, fought for his senses. He had brought Libba to Jonathan. Was his mission ended? He had hoped to bring her to God. He had hoped—but everything was collapsing.

Beyond a wall of flames, Libba collided with the young purser. He pushed her onto the deck. "Hurry, Miss. The pilot's ramming the boat ashore. When it strikes the bank, jump!"

"No!" she twisted away. "I can't go without Daniel." She searched a sea of smudged faces, shrieking, "Daniel!"

Flames leaped above the roof, met over the pilothouse. High in the air as if he were floating above them, the brave pilot remained at his post. The steamboat struck bank. Libba slammed to her knees.

Commands to jump ashore. Noise, confusion. Lily, Mignonne, Beau, her brother, Win. Hands picking Libba up, forcing her to make the terrifying leap.

Splashing, Libba hit cold water. Her hands went down, sank into oozing, muddy slime. All around her stunned passengers sat, crouched, knelt, in black swamp water. Wide-eyed they stared in helpless fascination at the flames engulfing the beautiful *Rebecca*. Hissing, sputtering, leaping, the fire consumed the boat to the water's edge.

In minutes, light, heat were gone. People were picking themselves up from the swamp, wading down the river toward a higher ridge of ground, shivering, suddenly realizing they were wet and cold.

The Chattahoochee was a solid sea of charred remnants. Fragmentary bales of burned cotton bobbed crazily in the currents. One bale washed ashore bearing a number of small coins, a bunch of keys, and three fingers of a human hand.

Horrified, Libba covered her face. A splashing in the dark water brought a relieved sigh from close beside her.

"Thank you, dear Lord," Lily Wingate prayed. "The officers are swimming to shore. I'm glad my Harrison wasn't with us. Captains always think they must save everyone or go down with their vessels."

Eyes straining, Libba leaned forward. Unable to breathe, she tried to distinguish the men rising like phoenix from the ash-laden water.

Cheers rang out because Pilot Lapham had managed to jump at the last minute. Captain Whitesides—the engineer—Paul, humbly accepting praise for heroism. Behind him a smaller man. The way he moved. It had to be. Daniel. Oh, yes, Daniel!

Blinded by tears, Libba struggled through the crowd. He was reaching out. His hands, his dear, sweet, funny face bore angry burns.

"Daniel!" She flung herself against him.

"Libba. Oh, my love!" He wrapped her in his arms as if he would never let her go. "I couldn't find you. I searched. So many staterooms separated us."

"Too many things have separated us!"

They drank in each other's aliveness, not worrying about decorum or people all around them. Suddenly Libba became aware that she and her clothes were wet and dirty, covered in mud. Embarrassed, she drew away from Daniel.

Paul touched her shoulder. "Thank God you're all right."

Wagons arrived from the Fitzgerald plantation, alerted by the glow from the holocaust. Davis Fitzgerald opened his home to all. Physicians came to help the many who were burned.

The remains of the hull had sunk, and none of the missing were found. After questioning his crew, the captain discovered that the globe had broken on the arc light. A spark from the electric light had ignited a ragged bale. Instead of smoldering, the tatters had been fanned into flames by the wind.

Libba listened through a haze of exhaustion. Her head nodded and her chin fell on her chest. She dozed, dreaming not of this fire but of turpentine and pine trees with railroad tracks twisted around them like pretzels.

"Libba."

She jerked upright. It was Paul standing before her. Somehow he had changed. His handsome face, his carriage had lost self-absorption, had taken on a new manhood.

"Yes, Paul?"

"I wanted to be certain you were all right before I left. Captain Whitesides and I are going to walk upriver and catch the train. I must telegraph the office. They will send another steamboat to fill the place of the *Rebecca*. The Chattahoochee has always been death for steamboats, but this disaster foreshadows the end of an era. The importance of the steamboat is breaking beneath the swift sure power of the railroads. Progress will win over romance." He took her hands in his with a rueful smile.

Libba wondered at the working of his face, the stiffening of his jaw as he shouldered responsibility. "I'm proud of you, Paul." Impulsively, she stood on tiptoe and kissed him goodbye.

Daniel, watching from across the way where a doctor was applying salve to his burns, saw only the kiss and thought forlornly, *She did not pull away from him. Libba has chosen Paul.*

nineteen

Sunlight burst through the mists of morning and streamed in the dormer window of Jonathan Ramsey's cottage in Eufaula where Libba sat writing. She turned words over on her tongue. With a sudden inspiration, she dipped her pen in the crystal inkwell.

> *Your tears that fall*
> > *to share my grief and shame,*
> *Say waters of*
> > *the world connect, and tears*
> *of one must cleanse*
> > *another's pain.*

She added the date, September 20, 1877. So much had happened in the past year. Yet everything that mattered had begun a few days ago. How exciting it was to express the freeing that forgiveness had brought her! She would make a gift of her poem to her father.

Probably she would never be a great poet, but this was the first step. Daniel's mother might even introduce her to Sidney Lanier.

Her heart was full of love to share. She wanted to spend time with her brother, to find out the ways he was different from and the ways he was a part of her, before she returned to Georgia. Everyone had invited her to stay in Eufaula, but she needed to share all that had happened with Miss Rebecca and Colonel Wadley and dear, dear Auntie.

Whistling drew her back to the window. Daniel was swinging through the gate carrying a mysterious package.

Scampering down the stairs, Libba flung open the door and dragged him into the parlor.

She wanted to throw her arms around him and kiss him. She had so much to tell him, but the way the outside corners of his eyebrows had gone up from his little-boy eyes made her stand back looking at him curiously.

"What have you brought me?"

Twisting his mobile face into a mocking expression, he spoke in a funny accent, "Who said this is for you?"

Libba stood on tiptoe to capture the brown-paper package he waved over her head. She untied the strings and blinked at a boxful of glazed German biscuits—pretzels.

"What?"

"I had a crazy idea. You'll think my parting gift silly, but I wanted to give you a good dream." He rubbed his hand over his hair, standing the gray strands in all directions. Libba had changed. She no longer looked weak and sick. Her eyes were sparkling like sunlight on clear water. She did not need to lean on him now. He longed to continue to hold her, but if he loved her enough to seek what was best for her, he must be ready to let her go. But how could he bear trusting her care to Paul? He must speak his piece and leave as quickly as possible.

Libba realized that Daniel was hurting. Why was he not sharing her happiness? She sat quietly waiting.

"I wanted to leave you with a different image of pretzels. A reminder to help you find the peace of forgiveness." He reddened. "People see pretzels as knots because they've forgotten their origin. Monks in southern Europe made them to reward children who learned their prayers. They represent a child's arms crossed in prayer. That's all you must do. Become as a child. Ask for forgiveness and give it—"

Libba stayed his words with a kiss. "You are a wonderful, caring man. I won't worry any more about deserving you. I'll just be thankful for being blessed." She laughed because he was puzzled. "You don't understand but how could you?"

Quickly she told Daniel about her experience during the fire. Beside him, she knew that all her searching was ended.

"Hatred and unforgiveness were blocking my heart, stopping my love from flowing. Now I know I loved you from the first moment you pulled me from the train wreck."

"*Me?* What about—I thought you'd decided on Paul!"

"Paul! How could you? Oh! You saw me kiss him goodbye. But I didn't think you'd think. . . . I was only congratulating him on growing up at last—and bidding him farewell. My darling, what I'd felt for Paul—before I really knew you, remember? That was only what some sage long ago termed puppy love."

Libba kissed Daniel with a passion that convinced him.

"Marry me now. There's a preacher in the other room."

Libba laughed shakily. "I'm sorry I've kept you waiting so long. But please. Just a little more patience. I promise to make the fastest wedding plans. . . . All of my best clothes burned, but I'll gather the quickest trousseau."

Suddenly love made her hungry. She bit a pretzel. "I won't forget what these mean."

A mischievous look crossed her face. "But can I still hate Sherman just a little?"

Daniel grinned and tousled her hair. "All sane men hate war. But just mentally. Don't let hatred and unforgiveness obsess you again. And after all, Sherman didn't defeat you. You and that spunky spirit rose up from the ashes the strong little person I could always see in there fighting. If you ever should have a nightmare again, you will be safely—" he knotted his arms around her, "wrapped in my love."

Libba and Daniel gazed from the windows of the belvedere of Barbour Hall for one last look across Eufaula and beyond the searching river.

Lily had wanted them to see the view from the widow's walk where she had watched for Harrison Wingate's steamboat, *Wave*, during that long ago time when the river had separated them. Libba smiled at Lily gratefully. Such a short while ago, these people had been strangers, but her step-mother Emma's nieces and nephews had included her in the circle of their love and now—glorious, glorious—she had a family.

Following Adrianna and Foy back down the winding stairs to the second floor, Libba and Daniel tiptoed into the nursery and stood over the cradle of Foy Edwards, Junior, in silent awe at the wonder of love. Libba reached out to touch Daniel's cheek with promise.

Libba leaned out the window of her bedroom at Great Hill Place. The sky was as clear and blue as only an October day could be. There remained no trace of September's fog. A train whistle floated across the peaceful woodland from Bolingbroke.

Endine flounced into the room. "The last of the guests have arrived. I never expected to see such a crowd of distinguished folks at the wedding of a couple of nobodies!"

Libba laughed. Secure now in her own identity, she could no longer be wounded by Endine. She was sorry that the girl was jealous. Her freckles had fairly stood out on stems since Libba's family jewels had been recovered. By piecing Papa's knowledge of the henhouse with Libba's remembrance of the jewel box's burial, they had been able to find the treasure and pay the taxes on Magnolia Springs. Papa joked that a burned-out plantation was a poor wedding gift, but Libba and Daniel knew that rich land waited for them to put down roots and grow.

Endine adjusted Libba's train, cascading like a waterfall of satin and Chantilly lace. Scallops of lace fell softly from her hands to reveal her treasured turquoise ring.

A tap sounded at the door. Colonel Wadley waited, stern-faced, but with love enough to spare for widows and orphans to be a father to her. Libba tried to express her thanks, but he shook his head and offered her his arm.

They descended the stone steps into the fragrant garden where Auntie had turned Hermes' secret place into a wedding bower.

Through a blur Libba saw Lily, Captain Wingate, Beau, and the lovely Mignonne. Happily, she smiled at Emma and Win, at Dorothea Marshall. Now the pathway had brought her at last to Daniel.

Unquestioning, they stepped before Jonathan Ramsey.

"Dearly beloved, we are gathered in the sight of God and these witnesses to join this man and this woman. . . ."

Daniel lifted the mists of her veil to kiss his bride. Her face was wet. Unashamed, Libba wept tears of joy.

acknowledgments

When readers asked for another book in my river series to tell what happened to Jonathan Ramsey's baby, it seemed impossible. How could I reunite them in an era when people rarely moved from their birthplaces? Although my main characters live only for my readers and me, my backgrounds are factual.

My search for this story was as circuitous as Libba's. Edward Mueller, author of *Perilous Journeys: A History of Steamboating on the Chattahoochee, Apalachicola, and Flint Rivers, 1828-1928*, told me the *Rebecca Everingham*, the grandest steamboat on the Chattahoochee, was named for a lady in Bolingbroke, Georgia. Kitty Oliver of the Middle Georgia Historical Society, introduced me to Rebecca Everingham Wadley's great-granddaughter, Mrs. Henry Dillon Winship. Anne Winship took me to Great Hill Place and made the era come alive. She entrusted me with Sarah Lois Wadley's diary, *A Brief Record of the Life of William Wadley*.

Libba's fiction and Wadley's fact melded. He oversaw the orphanage and did all I mentioned and much more. At a time when others of his era manipulated railroads to build wealth and power, Wadley worked on fixed principles of right and wrong that placed his company above his private interest. A bronze statue of Wadley, at Mulberry and Third in Macon, overlooks the railroads and river. With eyes seeming to snap and coattails seeming to flap, he remains a monument to railroading and to integrity.

I also thank poet Julia Evatt, who enticed me with the line, "Waters of the world connect." My excitement mounted at Ocmulgee National Monument with its use of words attributed to Chief Seattle: "All things are connected." Thanks to Sibbald Smith, Sam Lawson, and Sylvia Flowers. Thanks to Macon historian Calder W. Payne; Mrs. George G. Felton, Jr.; the Hay House Museum, which was Anne Johnson's home; and *Historical Record of Macon and Central Georgia* by Butler.

Thanks also go to *The First Hundred Years of Wesleyan College, 1836-1936* by Samuel Akers; to his widow, Elizabeth Akers, as well as to Miss Cornelia Shiver, Mrs. Schley Gatewood, Sr., and Joanne Weaver; to the Cowles Myles Collier Gallery at Wesleyan; to *Hope Bids Me Onward* by Castlen for the Shackelford story; to Libba Smith; to *The Story of Bulloch County;* to *War Is Hell,* Sherman; to Mary Burton Carson, who related my great-grandmother Rebecca Slaughter King's eyewitness account of the soldiers at Magnolia Springs; to Birdville Plantation; to Anne Rogers; to the Washington Memorial Library; to Harriet Bates, Lake Blackshear Regional Library; to Marty Willett and Nancy Gaston; to Glenda Calhoun; to Barbara Manger; to Carlene McPherson; and to Endine Hart.

The *Rebecca Everingham,* launched in 1880 and burned in 1884, signaled the end of the steamboat era on the Chattahoochee, but the romance of riverboats will never die.

Jacquelyn Cook

A Letter To Our Readers

Dear Reader:

In order that we might better contribute to your reading enjoyment, we would appreciate your taking a few minutes to respond to the following questions and return to:

Karen Carroll, Editor
Heartsong Presents
P.O. Box 719
Uhrichsville, Ohio 44683

1. Did you enjoy reading *Beyond the Searching River*?
   ❑ Very much. I would like to see more books by this author!
   ❑ Moderately
   ❑ I would have enjoyed it more if

   _____

2. Where did you purchase this book?_____

   _____

3. What influenced your decision to purchase this book?
   ❑ Cover   ❑ Back cover copy
   ❑ Title   ❑ Friends
   ❑ Publicity   ❑ Other _____

4. Please rate the following elements from 1 (poor) to 10 (superior).
   - ❏ Heroine   ❏ Plot
   - ❏ Hero   ❏ Inspirational theme
   - ❏ Setting   ❏ Secondary characters

5. What settings would you like to see in Heartsong Presents Books?

   _____

   _____

6. What are some inspirational themes you would like to see treated in future books?

   _____

   _____

7. Would you be interested in reading other Heartsong Presents Books?
   - ❏ Very interested
   - ❏ Moderately interested
   - ❏ Not interested

8. Please indicate your age range:
   - ❏ Under 18   ❏ 25-34   ❏ 46-55
   - ❏ 18-24   ❏ 35-45   ❏ Over 55

Name _____

Occupation _____

Address _____

City _____ State _____ Zip _____

LOVE A GREAT LOVE STORY?

Introducing Heartsong Presents —
Your Inspirational Book Club

Heartsong Presents Christian romance reader's service will provide you with four never before published romance titles every month! In fact, your books will be mailed to you at the same time advance copies are sent to book reviewers. You'll preview each of these new and unabridged books before they are released to the general public.

These books are filled with the kind of stories you have been longing for—stories of courtship, chivalry, honor, and virtue. Strong characters and riveting plot lines will make you want to read on and on. Romance is not dead, and each of these romantic tales will remind you that Christian faith is still the vital ingredient in an intimate relationship filled with true love and honest devotion.

Sign up today to receive your first set. Send no money now. We'll bill you only $9.97 post-paid with your shipment. Then every month you'll automatically receive the latest four "hot off the press" titles for the same low post-paid price of $9.97. That's a savings of 50% off the $4.95 cover price. When you consider the exaggerated shipping charges of other book clubs, your savings are even greater!

THERE IS NO RISK—you may cancel at any time without obligation. And if you aren't completely satisfied with any selection, return it for an immediate refund.

TO JOIN, just complete the coupon below, mail it today, and get ready for hours of wholesome entertainment.

Now you can curl up, relax, and enjoy some great reading full of the warmhearted spirit of romance.